METEORITE STRIKE

Behind them the night lit up a brilliant yellow. A split second later the sound of an explosion assaulted their ears. Through the swirling storm Sarah could see flames rising hundreds of feet into the air.

The plane had blown up.

Burning pieces of metal and debris fell through the air and landed all around. Suddenly, with the fire blazing high into the night, their present shelter didn't seem so safe. Daniel grabbed their arms and led them on into the darkness once more.

METEORITE STRIKE

A. G. TAYLOR

First published in the UK in 2010 by Usborne Publishing Ltd., Usborne House, 83-85 Saffron Hill, London EC1N 8RT, England. www.usborne.com

A CIP catalogue record for this book is available from the British Library.

JFMAMJJAS ND/09 94251 ISBN 9781409508571 Printed in Great Britain.

1

Nicole the air hostess was perfectly lovely: tall, thin and blonde with a calm voice that suggested she'd never raised it in her life. Sarah hated her from the moment they met.

"Hey, is that *Iron Man*? Cool movie."

"I've seen it twenty times," Robert replied, holding up the portable DVD player they'd been given for the flight. He seemed unaware of just how annoying Nicole was.

"Great," Nicole went on, flashing her blue eyes and leaning over Sarah to paw at the machine. "They've got *Wolverine* on the in-flight movies. You should check it out."

"We saw it in the cinema."

"I thought it was way better than the last *X-Men* film..."

Finally snapping, Sarah pushed Robert back a little too roughly, almost causing him to drop the player. He let out a cry of annoyance and the attendant looked at her in surprise.

"I know what you're doing," Sarah said flatly, meeting her eyes.

"I'm sorry?"

Sarah sighed loudly. "It's in your job description to make sure that the kids on your flight are having a *swell time*. Well, we're fine. So you don't have to pretend to be interested in what we're doing or what we have on our iPods."

"I just wanted to make sure—"

"If we want you, we'll press the button," Sarah interrupted, pointing to the panel in the handrest. "You don't have to keep bothering us."

Annoyance flashed in the woman's eyes. Then she put that fake smile back on her face for Robert's benefit.

"You want anything, just call, okay?" she said to him, talking past Sarah.

"Sure thing, Nicole."

"*Sure thing, Nicole*," Sarah mimicked under her breath as the woman walked away up the aisle of the plane. No doubt she was going back to the flight attendants' cubicle to tell them about the horrible girl in seat 28B. *Well, what do I care what she thinks?* Sarah thought angrily.

"Why were you so mean to her?" Robert asked, looking round with disapproval in his eyes.

"I hate adults like that. Ones who pretend to like all the same things you do. Wolverine *is cool. Justin is cool.* Yeah, right."

"I thought she was nice," Robert said, looking down at the player again. A lock of blond hair fell across his face and he brushed it out of his eyes with the back of his hand, just like Mum used to do with hers.

Sarah put her face close to his so she could make her point.

"She's paid to be nice, idiot."

Robert said nothing. He just put the headphones in his ears and started the movie again without even looking at her. Conversation over. He'd been doing that a lot recently. Sticking his face in the DVD player, the Nintendo or one of the other expensive toys he'd been bought whenever things got too difficult. Like things with Mum. Sarah knew from experience that he wouldn't even try to talk for another hour. *Fine.* She didn't want to hear how great Nicole was again, anyway.

"What are you two bickering about?"

Bickering? Eyebrows raised, Sarah looked across the aisle at the person who'd spoken.

"Bickering, Daniel?" she asked. "Just who says *bickering* any more?"

Daniel made a face and stroked a hand through his closely trimmed hair, just like he always did when he was annoyed and trying to hide it. In the month since he'd walked back into their lives, she'd picked up on that particular habit fast.

"I don't know, Sarah," he replied, mimicking her sarcastic tone. "I guess I must have heard it on an old, *old* TV show."

"Was it called *Ten Phrases for Wannabe Dads,* Daniel?" Sarah smirked, pleased with her own cleverness.

His jaw tightened visibly. "No, Sarah. I seem to remember it was called *Annoying Little—*"

Daniel stopped in mid-sentence, clearly with some effort. He placed a sleep mask over his eyes again and pushed his chair into the recline position.

"Wake me up when you're ready to be friendly," he said as he put in a set of earplugs.

Sarah opened her mouth to say something, but realized that it was useless. Both her travelling companions were dead to the world, cocooned in their little bubbles. Worst of all, she was stuck with them: an annoying kid brother and an equally annoying adult. If Mum were there on the plane it would have been okay, they could've talked, but she wasn't...Daniel was.

Daniel, their biological father (or *accidental dad*, as Sarah preferred to think of him), had walked out of their lives eight years before. After that, the most Sarah and Robert received from him every year were birthday and Christmas cards (usually bearing stamps from different parts of the world and containing American dollars that Mum would change at the bank).

Her memories of Daniel as a father were hazy, and for Robert, who was barely two years old when he left them, non-existent. There had been happy times, of course – Sarah remembered trips to the beach or the cinema as a family, before Robert had arrived. But those images were indistinct compared to the last one of Daniel and Mum arguing in the hall. There was a suitcase on the floor. Mum picked it up and threw it at him...

"If that's what you want, just get out, Daniel!"

Sarah often wondered what had really happened, but Mum had always refused to say – just that their dad had to leave because his work was on the other side of the world. But they'd been happy, hadn't they? She'd blamed Mum for a long time after Daniel left. Then she became angry at him. Then she didn't feel anything at all.

It was only when Mum became sick that Daniel returned – appearing off a long-haul flight from Australia four weeks before. Since then he'd been hanging around on the sidelines, having hushed conversations with Mum and the doctors when they all thought she wasn't listening. Sarah knew what the discussions were about, of course: what to do with them after Mum died.

Now, they were left with him...

Trying to tear her mind away from those thoughts, Sarah turned her attention to her television screen. Using the handset, she flipped to the flight progress channel. A misshapen white blob representing their plane was crossing a map of the world from England on the way to Australia. They'd already stopped in Hong Kong on the first part of the journey, which had taken almost thirteen hours. The map zoomed in and Sarah could see that they were now passing over the north-western part of Australia.

Almost two hours before, she and Robert had become excited when the map had finally shown the plane over

Australia. But looking out the window they'd only seen a lot of blackness. It was three in the morning local time, after all. For ages after that, there seemed to be no progress on the map whatsoever. Sarah was beginning to get the idea of just how big the country was when she looked at the remaining flight time. Their destination was Melbourne, in the south-east of the country, and there were still a few hours to go until they touched down there.

After a while Sarah gave up trying to see if the plane on the screen had moved. She was bored and there was nothing on the in-flight programme that she wanted to see. And fat chance of getting the DVD player away from Robert while he was watching *Iron Man* and in a sulk. She couldn't sleep either. Although her eyelids felt heavy, the constant hum of the engines kept her awake. This second part of the trip was starting to seem even longer than the first, she thought with a sigh.

Finally she decided to stretch her legs to relieve the boredom.

Pulling one of the headphones out of Robert's ear, she said, "I'm going for a walk. Don't get into trouble or Nicole will be very angry."

He stuck the headphone back and ignored her. Across the aisle, Daniel's head lolled against the side of his chair and he gave a low snore. Sarah shook her head at both of them and pushed herself up. Her legs felt stiff and she couldn't remember a time when she'd sat still for so long.

The lights of the cabin had been dimmed, creating a night-time effect to help the passengers sleep. Walking towards the middle of the plane Sarah had to be careful not to trip on people's feet sticking into the aisle. Most were sprawled in their chairs, some wearing eye masks and earplugs like Daniel, many of them snoring. At the other end of the cabin a baby was crying softly.

She stopped by the emergency exit and looked out of the window, hoping to see something out in the darkness. There was nothing. *Very exciting.*

It reminded her of sitting on the edge of Mum's bed in the hospital and being made to look at the Australia guidebook one of the nurses had brought in for them. Mum trying to tell her what an adventure it would be. Listing all the strange animals they only have in Australia. How in the outback you can go for hundreds of kilometres without passing through a town.

"It sounds boring," Sarah had said, looking away. "I'm not going."

"Sarah, please," Mum replied, putting a hand on her arm. "For Robert..."

He'd been sitting in the corner, plugged into a game on the Nintendo. If he could hear their conversation, he didn't show it.

"Everything I like is here. All my friends. School. Why is this happening?" Then she'd thrown her arms around Mum to hide the tears welling in her eyes.

"You've got to be strong for your brother," Mum whispered back. "I'm not going to be here much longer. Daniel...your dad is going to look after you. He wants to do the right thing this time..."

"And you believe that? He didn't want to eight years ago – not when his job was more important than us. Not when he wanted to follow it around the world and leave us behind."

"I've spoken to him and he's changed," Mum replied, taking her hand. "He's more...settled now. He's got a steady job and bought a house in Melbourne – somewhere you can all call home. I want you all to have a new start in Australia and so does Daniel, but he's going to need a lot of help."

"What about Monica?" Sarah protested. "Why can't we live with her?" Monica was Mum's boss and best friend. She had a big house in the city and a dog and Sarah got on well with her kids – well, most of the time...

"Monica has her own family to take care of," Mum said firmly. "We've been through this before. Daniel's your real dad and—"

"Beggars can't be choosers, right?" Sarah interrupted bitterly.

Mum sighed. "He wants another chance. Can you give him that, Sarah? For me?"

Sarah looked away, refusing to answer her mother for a long time.

"I'll help with Robert," she said finally, when it became clear Mum was prepared to wait all afternoon for an answer. "But I won't call him dad – ever. He'll just be a guy we're staying with until we're old enough to look after ourselves. That's the best I can do, okay?"

"Okay."

For a moment in the plane Sarah actually thought she might start crying again and quickly rubbed her eyes, worried that Nicole might come along and see her upset. The last thing she needed was more sympathy from a stranger. Nicole; the nurses at the hospital; Daniel; why couldn't they just mind their own business?

To clear her head, Sarah went through some of her warm-up exercises from the karate classes she'd been taking for the last two years. In the cramped space she even tried a few attacking stances to stretch her legs.

She would have attempted a couple of kicks but she was worried about hitting one of the chairs.

After five minutes she felt pleasantly out of breath and much more energized. Sarah leaned against the wall next to the stewards' station, a little cubicle where they all sat with the curtain drawn. The sound of a conversation reached her ears and before she knew it, she was listening in. The tones were hushed and unmistakeably anxious.

"...we going to have to turn back?" a male voice asked.

"Pete says that we should be okay," replied a woman Sarah recognized as Nicole. "But there's a cloud of dust the size of a city being blown to the south."

"What the hell will happen if we fly into it...?"

"They think it's going to bypass Melbourne. We can go around..."

"What about the airport? Sounds like it's going to be chaos..."

"And the news? Passengers will be seeing it on the in-flight TV when they wake up..."

Interested, Sarah moved a little closer, accidentally knocking the thin wall with her foot as she did so. The voices stopped. She stepped back as the curtain was drawn open.

"Anything wrong?" asked Nicole, calm as ever.

"I...I want a drink. Please."

Nicole looked back at the group huddled in the cubicle. Even in the dim light Sarah could see that the male attendant was white as a sheet.

"I'll bring it to you in a minute, Sarah. Go back to your seat, please."

"Is there something..."

"Go back to your seat."

Sarah turned and walked slowly back down the aisle, aware of Nicole watching as she went.

She found Robert asleep with the DVD still playing. As gently as possible, she pulled the headphones from his ears and turned off the machine to save the battery. Then she started flicking through the in-flight TV to find a news channel. It didn't take long before she'd found what had worried Nicole and the others so much.

An American station was showing satellite footage of what looked like a cloud passing through the centre of Australia. Based on her knowledge of the size of the place, Sarah could see that it must be huge. A headline running across the bottom of the screen read:

BREAKING NEWS: METEORITE HITS CENTRAL AUSTRALIA. EMERGENCY SERVICES ON

HIGH ALERT. HUNDRED-KILOMETRE-WIDE DUST CLOUD SPREADING.

Sarah's mouth went dry. They were flying straight towards it.

2

"I want some answers and I want them now!" a man's voice demanded, loud enough to make heads turn along the cabin.

The passengers had started waking up in the half hour since Sarah returned to her seat. Things got interesting once they started checking out the news reports on the in-flight TV. Word of the disaster spread like a virus. People shuffled in their seats, had whispered conversations and rang buzzers for the flight attendants up and down the aisles. Sarah was almost glad of something to relieve the boredom of the long night. Robert woke up and for once didn't start straight back into one of his films.

"What's going on, Sarah?" he asked, tugging on her arm as she craned her head past the seat to see what was going on. A few rows back, a man stood in front of the white-faced male attendant, screaming abuse while his wife tried to calm him down.

"Sarah!"

She half-turned back to Robert.

"It's okay, nothing's happening," she said. "Watch another DVD or play a game."

Her brother narrowed his eyes, just like he always did when he wasn't going to take "no" for an answer. At ten, Robert was almost four years younger than Sarah, but she realized he wasn't stupid.

"Okay, okay," she said, flipping the TV to the news station. "There's been a meteor crash. It hit somewhere in the middle of Australia. You know what a meteor is?"

"Of course I do," Robert said, rolling his eyes. "A lump of rock flying through space. And if it's crashed to earth it's called a meteorite, actually. Miss Dobson says..."

Sarah could tell Robert was about to go into one of his speeches about what his teacher said on a subject, which he did from time to time. She always teased him about being in love with Miss Dobson, which drove him nuts.

"Fine, you know more about it than I do," she said, putting on the cheap, chunky headphones the attendants had provided rather than listen to her brother go on.

On the news, the presenters were doing much the same things they had been doing fifteen minutes before: watching the satellite footage, making guesses about the size of the cloud and repeating numbers for people to call. She got the feeling they really didn't have that much new information to give.

Robert tugged on her arm again and she pulled off the headset with a look of annoyance.

"I don't like it, Sarah," he said, a note of fear in his voice.

Behind them the voices had gone up a notch in volume. The angry man was still shouting and some other passengers had joined in. Nicole was trying to calm everyone down. It didn't seem to be working.

Across the aisle, Sarah saw Daniel also turn in his seat. He'd finally taken off his mask and removed the ear plugs. He rolled his eyes at her and shook his head.

"Some people, eh?"

The Aussie lilt to his accent still sounded alien to her. How could they have a dad who spoke like that? And he dressed dorky too, in a jacket and shirt that made him look like an elderly professor, although Sarah knew he wasn't that old.

"Make them stop shouting, Sarah," Robert whined, grabbing at her arm. She was about to turn and tell him to shut up when Daniel leaned across the aisle and offered something to him.

"Do you like kangaroos?"

Robert looked at him, a little taken aback. He'd kept his distance from Daniel since their first meeting in the hospital, instinctively mistrusting anyone who was an adult and not Mum.

"Sure, I guess," he said after a moment. "I've never seen one for real." He took the object from Daniel's hand.

"Those are my photos," Daniel said. "I've seen loads. Was going to give them to you when we reached Melbourne, but perhaps you'd like to see them now."

Robert started leafing through the little album and Sarah looked too, despite herself. The photos showed shot after shot of kangaroos in the wild, probably taken out in the bush somewhere.

"Cool," whispered Robert. "Could you feed them?"

"No, those were wild animals," Daniel explained. "But if you keep flipping there are some pics that were taken when I visited one of the wildlife parks. You can buy a bag of food and they eat from your hand."

"Wow. Look at the size of that spider!"

"Yeah, that was a huntsman I snapped when I was camping. It was as big as my hand, but it's the little ones you have to watch out for really. Some of them can kill a man with their venom. Hold on to the album for a while."

With that, Daniel sat back in his seat with a wink to Sarah. Engrossed in the pictures, Robert had completely forgotten the noise of the arguing passengers. Sarah had to admit it had done the trick and she felt she owed Daniel something, against her better judgement.

"Thanks," Sarah said quickly as she looked back up the aisle.

Daniel smiled at her. "No worries. I'm sure it's going to be okay. You don't have to be afraid."

"Who said I was afraid?" she replied defensively, suddenly regretting trying to be nice to him after all. Clearly he still thought she was six years old.

She was about to say something more when, without warning, the dimmed cabin lights flicked on at full power. A calm voice of authority from the cabin speaker cut through the noise.

"This is your captain speaking... Please could all

passengers return to their seats and fasten their seat belts. Stand by for another announcement."

Silence fell in the cabin. People who were out of their seats quickly returned to their places and sat quietly, as if they'd been told off by a teacher. Up and down the plane, seat belts clicked as they were fastened. The attendants walked back towards the middle of the plane, in control again. Nicole looked a little red-faced following the disagreement, Sarah noted.

A minute later the speaker delivered another message.

"This is Captain Klein... As you're probably all aware, there's been an incident below us. At present I can't give you too much information about the meteorite. If you've been watching the news, you probably know as much as I do. All I can tell you is that you're in the safest place right now. We're either going to fly round or over the dust cloud, but even if we do have to go through for a while, our GPS system will keep us right on track."

Someone down the front of the plane let out a cheer and a ripple of applause spread down the aisles. Sarah stole a look at Daniel. Although he was listening intently to the message, she noticed he wasn't clapping.

"We're expecting to land in Melbourne in just over two and a half hours. Until then, I'd like all passengers to

refrain from using mobile phones and keep seat belts on. There's been some magnetic disturbance due to the impact and we don't want to take any chances. The cabin crew are now going to run through emergency procedures once more. So sit back, stay calm and we'll be in Melbourne before you know it."

There was more applause, a little quieter this time. The flight attendants started demonstrating where the emergency exits were, like they had done at the start of the flight. Everyone seemed to be paying attention this time.

Sarah looked over at Daniel, who was frowning.

"Is there something wrong?" she asked after a moment.

He looked round at her, as if surprised that she had spoken to him.

"Oh... It's nothing..."

Sarah sighed and leaned a little closer so that Robert couldn't hear.

"Stop treating me like a kid, okay?" she said quietly. "You weren't clapping like everyone else. Why?"

He looked at her for a moment, as if considering carefully what he said next.

"If anything happens, you and Robert stick close to me."

"What do you mean, if anything happens?"

Daniel glanced up the aisle to where Nicole was demonstrating how to put on one of the oxygen masks.

"It's probably nothing," he said casually, looking away. "Better safe than sorry."

It was then that Sarah realized something important. Daniel thought the plane was going to crash.

3

When things started to go wrong, it happened so quickly nobody seemed to know what to do.

The cabin quietened down following the captain's announcement. People stayed in their seats and stopped demanding information from the attendants. Most of them seemed totally engrossed in what was on the news channels, although from what Sarah could see there wasn't much new information there. A few people talked and laughed as if nothing strange was happening at all.

Robert soon lost interest in what was going on and started watching *Finding Nemo* for the millionth time.

Sarah picked up the forgotten photo album from the side of his chair and leaned across the aisle to give it back to Daniel. To her surprise, he had his mobile phone open and was writing a text. She craned her head round to see what he was writing: FLGT PROB – PCKGE SAFE – WILL DLIVER, DELAY POSS.

"Hey, you're not supposed to be doing that," she said, causing him to look round in surprise.

He shrugged and angled the screen so she couldn't read any more. "I don't think one text's going to make any difference, do you?"

"What if everyone on the plane thought that?"

"Well, I'm not everyone." Daniel took the album from her hand with a wink and pressed *send* on the phone.

A shudder passed through the plane and the cabin jerked to the right, throwing Sarah forward. Daniel reached out and caught her arm. If she hadn't been strapped in she might have fallen into the aisle.

The plane righted itself and they met each other's eyes.

"Just a little turbulence," Daniel said, grinning. She laughed, almost forgetting that she disliked him.

"Hey!" Robert cried out beside her. Sarah looked

round and saw that the DVD player in his lap had gone dead.

The plane shuddered again, this time so violently that some of the overhead lockers sprang open, spilling cabin baggage onto the heads of passengers. The whole cabin rolled to the right, sending loose objects flying through the air.

Sarah held on to the arm of the chair, steadying Robert with her other hand. She met his eyes and saw he was terrified. She was about to tell him not to worry when the lights in the cabin went out.

Up and down the aisles people started screaming. At the other end of the plane something heavy crashed down and a woman cried out. Two seconds later the lights flicked on again, only much dimmer, making it difficult to see exactly what was going on.

"This is your Captain..." the speaker began and then abruptly crackled and died.

Sarah felt her stomach sink, just like it had when the plane approached the airport in Hong Kong. However, this time the feeling was much stronger and more sudden. The plane was descending – fast. The engines roared with a deafening intensity. She looked round at Daniel.

"What's happening?" she shouted above the din.

“We’re going to land!” he called back.

“We can’t land!” she cried, knowing it sounded stupid. “We’re not at the airport yet!”

Daniel shook his head and motioned downwards with his finger. “Bend over and put your head between your legs. Put your hands over your head or hold the seat in front. Tell Robert to do the same.”

With that, he unclipped his seat belt and reached up to grab a bag from the overhead locker. Sarah hastily told Robert what to do and did the same herself, watching Daniel from the corner of her eye. He pulled a silver glasses case from his bag, as if to check it was okay. Satisfied, he replaced the case and stuffed the bag under his seat before buckling his seat belt. Sarah frowned – she had never seen Daniel wear glasses. As he glanced in her direction, she looked away. Sarah had the strangest feeling she’d seen something she shouldn’t.

However, there was no time to think about that. The feeling of rapid descent intensified, as if the plane was rushing towards the ground even more quickly. Luggage and objects that had fallen out of the lockers were sliding down the aisle towards the front. Stealing a look round the chair, Sarah saw Nicole strapping herself into a little seat that folded down from the wall.

"This is it!" Daniel yelled as the cabin levelled out, as if the pilot had managed to raise the nose of the plane. The engines roared even louder, drowning out all other sound in the cabin.

An impact juddered through the entire plane, causing Sarah to jump in her seat and then come back down again so violently she bit her lip. It was as if the plane had hit something and then bounced back up in the air. She wiped her mouth, tasting blood, and looked round at Robert. He had his head between his knees but his whole body was shaking. She reached over and put an arm round his shoulders.

The plane hit the ground again, harder this time, and kept moving for a few seconds. *We'll be okay*, Sarah found herself thinking. She remembered pictures of the desert in Australia, so flat and empty. Probably not that much different from landing at an airport, just a few more bushes and rocks to look out for. Right?

From beneath the floor of the cabin came the terrible sound of metal tearing and then another impact. On the left side of the plane something exploded with an almighty booming sound. At the edge of her vision, Sarah saw fire leap up at the window.

Suddenly the whole cabin seemed to spin round to the right, as if the plane was now sliding along sideways rather than forwards. The sound of the engines had lessened and Sarah could hear the cries of the other passengers once again. The walls and floor were shaking so violently, she wondered if the whole cabin was going to split apart and spill them out into the desert.

Then, just as suddenly as the ordeal had begun, it ended.

With a heavy thud, the plane came to a halt, rolled a little to the right and then settled back at a slight angle. The interior fell silent for a moment as people unfolded themselves and looked around, amazed they were in one piece. Sarah looked up the aisle and saw Nicole hastily unbuckling herself from her seat. The woman moved to the exit door and started operating the emergency release handles.

Sarah unclipped her own belt and turned to Robert, who was looking back at her with tear-stained eyes.

"Is it over?" he asked, voice very small.

Sarah nodded and ran a hand through his hair, just like she'd seen Mum do the time he fell off his bike and cut open his knee.

"We're going to be okay," she told him.

All around, people were struggling out of their seats and rushing into the aisles, heading for the doors. A bottleneck quickly formed, with people at the back pushing and shouting as they desperately tried to get to the exits. *So much for an orderly evacuation,* thought Sarah. She started to move as well, grabbing Robert's hand, but Daniel shook his head at her.

"Wait, Sarah!" he called. "You'll get trampled by these idiots."

Sure enough, so many people were trying to pile into the aisle at once that they were starting to fall over the top of each other in their haste. Some of them were nursing wounded arms and heads from the crash. They stepped on one another in the confusion. Robert gripped Sarah's arm tighter.

Sarah looked back to where Nicole was heaving open the emergency door, while another attendant tried to hold people back for a moment. And that's when it happened...

The door swung open and a cloud of choking red dust flooded into the cabin, driving people back down the aisles. Outside a storm was raging and now it invaded the plane. Too late, Sarah raised a hand to her face and got a mouthful of the sandy dust as the cloud enveloped her seat. She bent forward, coughing and rubbing her eyes.

Seconds before, people had been desperately rushing towards the doors, but now they struggled back, away from the dust storm that was tearing through the cabin. *We must have landed in the cloud*, Sarah thought to herself as she shielded Robert's face and looked round at the panicking passengers through watery eyes.

"Come on," a voice ordered. She looked up to see Daniel standing beside her seat, a handkerchief held over his nose and mouth to stop the dust. From his shoulder bag he produced a T-shirt that he ripped into two pieces and handed to her.

"Hold this over your face."

She took the material gratefully and gave the other piece to Robert.

"We can't go out there," she protested as Daniel started pulling her to her feet. "We're in the cloud!"

"We can't stay here," he said, looking round as someone pushed past him roughly. People were piling up at the back of the plane now, trying to get as far from the open door as possible.

"We can't breathe out there!" Sarah argued, pulling away violently.

Daniel bent his face close to her ear, so Robert couldn't hear.

"This plane is going to explode. The engine is on fire. Do you understand?"

Sarah met his eyes for a second and could see that he was deadly serious. Through the nearest window yellow flames were visible in the storm. She said nothing, merely nodded.

Daniel took her arm again and led her up the aisle while she held onto Robert's hand, shielding their faces as much as possible as they went. The door was stuck open and the inside of the plane was slowly filling with more and more red dust. It swirled in the air and settled over the floor and seats, giving everything a strange, brownish hue.

At the door, Nicole stood with her hands covering her face. She was dust-covered and almost unrecognizable. She waved them back as they approached.

"Wait...!" she cried, stepping forwards.

Daniel ignored her, pulling them to the edge of the doorway where the storm was raging with massive intensity. On the threshold Sarah resisted, holding Robert to her. She almost lost the piece of T-shirt and got another mouthful of dust, making her retch. *This was madness.* She turned to protest.

Too late! Daniel pushed her in the small of the back and she toppled forward, pulling Robert with her.

She expected to fall, but instead hit the rubbery surface of an inflatable emergency chute and slid forwards. It was like being on a funfair slide for an exhilarating few seconds.

They hit the sand and rolled forwards, tumbling over each other in the dark.

"Come on!" Daniel cried, landing behind them. "Don't stop moving!"

He pulled them onward again, only this time in the darkness they couldn't see where they were going. Robert started sobbing, but Sarah didn't let go of his hand.

They went on, stumbling over the uneven ground and tripping on plants for what seemed like an age before Daniel finally stopped. He hauled them down next to a ridge that provided a little shelter from the storm.

In the darkness Sarah could just make out the faces of her brother and Daniel as they crouched close together. The cold was starting to bite through her jumper and she realized that she'd left her coat in the plane.

"I think we're far enough away!" Daniel yelled over the wind.

Sarah felt a surge of anger rise. They could have stayed in the cabin. It would have to be safer than being stuck out in the dark, cold and dust of the desert. Mum would never have put them in such danger! Some father Daniel was turning out to be! She opened her mouth to tell him she was going back and taking Robert with her—

Behind them the night lit up a brilliant yellow. A split second later the sound of an explosion assaulted their ears. Through the swirling storm Sarah could see flames rising hundreds of feet into the air.

The plane had blown up.

Burning pieces of metal and debris fell through the air and landed all around. Suddenly, with the fire blazing high into the night, their present shelter didn't seem so safe. Daniel grabbed their arms and led them on into the darkness once more.

For what seemed like an age, they fought their way through the storm.

Finally, more from exhaustion than anything else, they collapsed against another ridge. The dusty vortex of the storm howled all around.

There was nothing to do but huddle close to wait for the dawn.

4

At some time during the night, Sarah must have fallen asleep, because she woke to find the darkness had passed. Above them the sky was obscured by a layer of dull, reddish-looking cloud through which the sun shone faintly, creating a strange kind of twilight at dawn.

She got stiffly to her feet and looked down at her clothes, which were covered in a thick layer of sand and dust. She brushed it away as best she could, in the process creating a cloud that made her cough.

Over to her left, Sarah saw Robert sitting on a rock

with the portable DVD player cradled protectively in his lap. His face and hair were covered in dust, giving him the appearance of a desert ghost.

"It doesn't work any more," he said, holding up the DVD player as she approached.

"The batteries must be flat," Sarah replied. She stood on the rock next to him and looked around.

In every direction there was sandy flatness, the only vegetation being shrubs and low-lying trees. Perhaps a kilometre or so away, a column of thick, black smoke was rising into the air. The plane.

"They're not flat," Robert said, matter-of-factly. "The battery warning light would be flashing. And it isn't flashing."

Sarah looked round at him, amazed that he could fuss about one of his precious gadgets after everything that had happened. Just a few hours before he'd been unable to stop crying. She guessed she should be relieved. He was acting normal...for him.

"It's probably been knocked out by an electro-magnetic pulse," Daniel said, walking out of the desert behind them.

"Yeah, EMP," agreed Robert. "Of course."

"What?" asked Sarah, looking round.

"Some kind of residual effect of the meteorite strike,"

Daniel explained as he fished a couple of water bottles from his shoulder bag and tossed them over. "An EMP can knock out all electronic equipment for miles. My phone isn't working either and it's probably what brought the plane down."

EMP? Residual effect? Sarah thought Daniel was starting to sound more like Robert every minute.

She opened her bottle and drank half of it quickly, realizing just how dry her throat was. Already the cool of the night was being replaced with a warmth that would only get stronger as the day went on. Sarah had read in the guidebook that desert temperatures could easily reach fifty degrees.

"Where have you been?" she asked Daniel as he sat down on the rock and swigged from a bottle of his own.

"Just looking around," he replied.

"At the plane?"

He shook his head. "No, I was just going to head back there. It should be okay."

"I'm coming with you," said Sarah.

"Me too!" added Robert.

Daniel stood and shook his head. "Uh-uh. Too dangerous. You two stay here and wait for me."

He hitched his bag on his shoulder and began to move off in the direction of the rising smoke. Sarah jumped round to block his path.

"Hold it," she said. "We're going too."

"No, you're not," he answered and stepped around her. "Wait here. I'll be one hour."

"You can't stop us from coming with you," Sarah said sharply, moving to block him again.

They faced each other in silence for a moment, at a stand-off. From his rock, Robert watched them both, clearly interested to see who would win the dispute.

Finally, Daniel shrugged and stood to one side.

"Fine. Come then."

He readjusted his shoulder bag and set off again. Sarah and Robert exchanged a surprised look. Getting Mum to give up on an issue had never been so easy.

"Well, get a move on!" Daniel called over his shoulder and they ran to catch up.

Finding the crash site again wasn't difficult. The smoke could probably be seen for hundreds of kilometres in this flat landscape. Earlier Sarah had regretted leaving her coat on the plane in the panic to escape, but now she found herself sweating with the rising heat and the effort required to walk through the red, shifting sand.

The landscape looked exactly like the pictures of the outback she'd seen in books and films about Australia. Except those images hadn't done justice to the openness and the emptiness of everything. It gave her the feeling of being a tiny speck in a vast expanse. She wondered how far they were from Melbourne. Or even the nearest town.

"Where's the sun?" Robert asked, walking along with his face to the sky, almost tripping over in the process. Above them there was no gap in the rust-coloured clouds.

"The dust thrown up by the meteorite has settled in the atmosphere," Daniel explained, not looking round or breaking his stride. He was setting a fast pace and hadn't stopped to check if they were managing to keep up. Obviously he just expected they would because they'd asked to come.

"We might not see the sun for days," he added. "Perhaps if there's rain it might help settle some of the debris."

"What are you, a geography teacher?" Sarah said with an edge in her voice, trying to disguise the fact that she was a little out of breath.

Daniel looked round, but he had a smile on his face. "Engineer, actually. I think I mentioned it a couple of times before."

Sarah replied sarcastically, "Sorry, I forgot you have a really cool job. Wow."

Robert brushed past her and ran up beside Daniel. "Hey, I've been meaning to ask you..."

Sarah sighed as Robert proceeded to bombard Daniel with a thousand questions about his work, just like he always did when something caught his interest. She hung back and drank the rest of her water, slowing her pace a little to save energy. She watched her younger brother looking up to the man they were supposed to call their father as he spoke, enthralled by what Daniel had to say. Something inside her turned over as she realized that it probably wouldn't be too difficult for Robert to accept Daniel back as his dad. He was younger. And a boy. They could always find boy stuff to do together. But where did that leave her?

"Hey, don't fall behind," Daniel called to her, looking back and slowing so she could catch up. "You're the one who wanted to go back to the plane so badly."

"I don't care about going back to the plane," she said, aware that her voice had taken on a nasty edge. "I just didn't want you leaving us alone in the desert and not coming back."

Daniel frowned as she walked up beside him. "I was worried there might be another explosion and there could be some things at the crash... Let's just say, it might not be pretty and I didn't want you two seeing something bad." He paused for a moment. "Do you really think I'd desert you?"

"Why not?" replied Sarah. "You've left us before! Perhaps you were thinking that you didn't need two kids to look after. What better place to lose us than the outback?"

They walked on, watching Robert, who had run on ahead and was struggling up a little hill of sand.

"I haven't been there, you're right," Daniel admitted. "And I haven't earned the right to call myself a dad yet. But I'm not about to abandon you, Sarah. And as for looking after you and Robert, I think you're doing a good enough job of that yourself."

Sarah didn't say anything for a moment.

"Robert likes you," she told him finally.

"Yeah?" Daniel said. "How do you feel?"

Sarah thought about it. "You did pretty well getting us off that plane."

Daniel looked like he was going to say something else, but stopped short when Robert let out a cry from the top of the ridge of sand. Despite the heat, they ran to catch up with him. At the top of the little hill, they saw what he was looking at.

A groove, hundreds of metres long, had been scraped into the desert floor, stretching away into the distance.

It had clearly been made by the plane as it hit the ground for the first time. Directly ahead, one of the plane's landing wheels and its torn metal strut were half-buried in the sand.

Suitcases, backpacks and boxes littered the ground, some of them ripped open, spilling their contents. There were dozens.

Daniel clapped a hand on Robert's shoulder and started down the ridge towards the nearest case.

"Jackpot!" he cried, his voice suddenly full of excitement. "Looks like it's our lucky day. The cargo hold must've split open when we first hit."

For a moment Robert and Sarah didn't move.

"I have a bad feeling about this," she said, staring at the belongings scattered randomly across the dunes. They looked like alien artefacts strewn about the sand. *Where are their owners now?* she wondered. The thought wasn't a pleasant one.

"Come on," she said and they started down the dune after Daniel.

5

"Hey, what are you doing?" Sarah cried, running down the last few metres of the ridge. "That's not your stuff!"

Daniel kneeled over one of the open suitcases, rummaging through the contents. Clothes and books flew out onto the sand. Finally, he extracted a little first-aid kit and stuffed it into his bag.

"I said, what are you doing?" Sarah demanded, standing over him.

Daniel stood and moved to the next case, a few metres away on the sand.

"What does it look like? I'm collecting things that could be useful."

"It looks like you're stealing from people's cases," Sarah replied, following him.

"Well if I see the people these things belong to, I'll be sure to give them right back," Daniel said as he ripped open the straps on the next case and started tossing out clothes. He looked round at Robert, who was standing over to one side. "Hey, Bobbie! Empty out that bag next to you and see if there's anything we can use."

"Okay!"

Nobody other than Mum called her brother *Bobbie*, but from Daniel he didn't seem to mind. Sarah looked in amazement as her brother unquestioningly started working through someone else's suitcase, throwing things out on the sand in the same manner as Daniel. She ran and stood over him.

"Stop it, Robert," she ordered.

He ignored her, digging deeper into the suitcase.

"Stop it!"

More clothes went flying.

"I said, stop it!"

She grabbed the case and tried to pull it away from him. Robert pulled back with all his strength, his face suddenly angry as he looked up at her.

"Cut it out, Sarah!"

She let go and Robert fell back onto the ground heavily, the suitcase on top of him.

"Mum wouldn't like this," Sarah said angrily. "She said she'd watch over us after she died, you know. She can see everything you're doing."

She regretted saying it immediately. Tears welled in her brother's eyes, but he rubbed them away with his dusty hands and struggled to his feet.

"Mum would want us to be safe," he said defiantly. Reaching into the suitcase, he produced a baseball cap and handed it to her. "You'll need it for when the sun comes back."

Sarah stepped away, the fight draining from her. She sat down on a red suitcase as Robert went to work on a large rucksack. She watched her brother in silence for a while, turning the cap over in her hands.

"How about these?" Robert called out, holding up a box of aspirin and a blanket.

"Great!" Daniel shouted back. "And bring over an empty backpack too. We can use it to carry stuff."

Sarah watched them working for another moment before coming to a decision. She got up, flipped open the case she'd been sitting on and ran a hand over the neatly folded clothes within – everything packed for a holiday in the sun. She didn't find too much of interest apart from a bottle of sunscreen. If the clouds ever cleared, they would need it. She took the bottle and closed the case.

Moving on, Sarah opened the next case and the next, taking only what she thought would be useful. Pretty soon, however, she forgot that they belonged to other people and was ripping them open with as much eagerness as Daniel and her brother.

After fifteen minutes they had a little pile of blankets, first-aid equipment and toiletries. Daniel started putting what they had found into the new backpack and gave Robert his own bag to carry, pulling out a couple of objects before he did so. They had also found several chocolate bars, cans of drink and other food. These things Daniel put into the shoulder bag. One item he kept for himself: a bottle of whisky that he placed in his jacket pocket. He caught them watching him critically.

"Hey!" he protested. "For medicinal purposes, okay?"

"Right," Sarah replied, folding her arms. Daniel shrugged and hoisted the pack onto his back.

"Okay, let's go," he said. "We'll see what we can find at the crash site and then carry on."

"Carry on?" asked Sarah, half running to keep up with him.

"To the nearest town," Daniel explained. "Then hopefully on to Melbourne. If we can find a car that works, that is."

"I bet you'll be able to fix it if it doesn't," Robert said eagerly and Daniel ruffled his hair.

"Don't you think we should stay by the plane?" Sarah asked uncertainly. "I mean, won't they be looking for us? Rescuers, I mean."

Daniel shrugged. "Maybe. Or maybe not. Who knows how many planes went down? Or even if they can get here? It might take days or weeks."

"But the nearest town might be hundreds of kilometres away."

"Then we'll have a long walk, won't we?"

Sarah fell silent at the thought.

With another five minutes' walk, the rising smoke started to fill the horizon. Crossing another incline, they saw the wreck of the plane spread out before them. The central section of the fuselage had split open and was still burning in places. The nearest wing had fallen off and the two jet engines were no more than smoking shells. The tail of the plane was ripped away and nowhere to be seen.

"Wow," Robert said quietly at the sight before them.

"You said it," agreed Daniel as they started forward.

"We could've been trapped in there," Sarah said to herself as she looked at the scene below. Around the edge of the wreck she could see the burned remains of seats and luggage from the plane. Looking more closely, she made out blackened shapes: the bodies of those passengers who hadn't made it out before the explosion. Sarah turned her head away from the horrible image and concentrated on the scene closer to them.

All around on the sand in front of the plane, survivors were lying in groups, huddled together, dust- and soot-covered. Robert moved closer to Sarah. He put his hand in hers as they passed a family lying on the ground, sleeping soundly. There was something odd about seeing them stretched out in the open, having made no attempt even to cover or protect themselves.

Looking around, Sarah noticed that most of the survivors were doing the same. It was as if they'd walked out of the plane and slept where they had fallen. A hundred people at least. Here and there people wandered amongst the sleeping survivors, but there weren't many on their feet – twenty at most. These passengers looked dazed, as if unsure about what had happened or where they were. In fact, they seemed on the verge of collapse themselves.

"Stay close to me," Daniel said as they made their way carefully through the crowds of sleeping people.

"Are they dead, Sarah?" Robert asked at her side.

Sarah shook her head. "No, they're breathing – asleep. I guess everyone's resting after the crash." She had to admit, it didn't sound very convincing.

Looking around, she could have cried at what she saw. Injured people stripped of their belongings lay on the bare earth, some of them holding on to each other, some snoring quietly. In the distance she made out the familiar face of Nicole, the flight attendant, bandaging a sleeping man's arm and suddenly wished she hadn't been so horrible to her earlier. She'd only been doing her job, after all.

A man in a white shirt approached them through the people. Sarah recognized him as Captain Klein. He'd walked through the cabin during the flight, saying hello to several of the passengers as he did. Now his hair was a mess and his perfectly ironed uniform was dirt-smeared and torn in places. A blue pilot's jacket hung loosely from his shoulders like a cape and he staggered a little when he walked. Klein's eyes were bloodshot and looked heavy, as if he hadn't slept for a week.

When he saw them he held up a hand, waving them back.

"Don't come any closer!" he ordered, his voice cracking a little with stress.

Daniel put out an arm to stop them moving forward.

"What's going on, Captain?" he called out.

"People are getting sick," Klein replied, rubbing his eyes, as if it were a massive effort just keeping them open. "Must be something in the dust...making us sleep..."

Without warning, the captain fell to one knee, as if it were suddenly too much effort to stand upright.

"If you're not feeling it yet, get as far away from here as possible," he said, staring at them desperately. "Don't come near us. It seems to be contagious."

Sarah felt Robert gripping her arm so tightly she thought his nails might tear into her skin. Daniel ushered them both back.

"We're leaving," he said quietly. "Now."

"But we have to help..." Sarah objected.

Daniel caught her arm. "There's nothing we can do. Come on, quickly."

Sarah pulled herself free of his grasp and ran towards the sleepers before he could grab her again.

"I said, we have to help," she repeated, kneeling by the nearest group of people. It was a family by the looks of it: mum, dad and two kids. She placed a hand on the man's shoulder and shook him. He seemed to stir in his sleep momentarily, letting out a deep breath, but then remained motionless. Undeterred, Sarah moved on to the woman, shaking her more roughly.

"Hey, wake up!" she shouted at the sleeper. "You're going to die out here!"

There was no response. Sarah let the woman go and sat down on the sand. The sleeper's head fell back, mouth open, exposed. Sarah looked away.

"Sarah, get away from her," Daniel called over. "He said they're infectious."

"Come on," Robert added, fear in his voice. "Maybe Daniel's right."

She looked round at Captain Klein, who was watching the scene on his knees a few metres away. Sarah felt a sudden surge of anger at seeing him there, defeated when he should be taking charge of the whole mess. She stumbled over and pulled at his arm in an effort to rouse him.

"Help us!" she demanded. "You're the captain. You've got to do something!"

Klein looked up at her and she saw the desperation in his eyes.

"I'm sorry, I..." he replied, his voice barely a whisper as he fell back on the sand. Sarah placed a hand on his arm, but the pilot didn't move. Swallowing hard, she shifted him onto his back and picked up his fallen jacket, rolling it into a ball and placing it under his head like a pillow. She really couldn't think of anything else to do.

Sarah rose to her feet slowly. She walked back in silence to where Daniel and her brother were waiting.

"What's going on?" she asked desperately.

"I'm sorry, Sarah, I really don't know," Daniel replied gently. "But we have to get out of here. Whatever's causing this could be spreading. Do you understand?"

She nodded reluctantly and allowed him to steer her and Robert from the crash site.

"You did a good job landing the plane, Captain," Daniel called back as they walked away. Captain Klein gave no indication he'd heard.

Atop the ridge they took a moment to look back.

A hundred people slept on the sand amidst the broken seats and luggage that had been thrown from the plane. It was as if a magic wand had been passed over them like in some fairy tale.

Yet this was deadly serious.

"Come on," Daniel said, pulling Robert away.

Taking a final look back, Sarah saw a few of the passengers still moving among the sleepers. She looked around for Nicole, but she was no longer anywhere to be seen. For a moment, Sarah wondered if they should go back for her and the others, but realized that Daniel was right: they had to get away from the crash site as fast as possible before they ended up as sleepers too.

Tearing her eyes away from the chilling scene, Sarah hurried down the other side of the ridge after Daniel and her brother.

6

Even after two hours' walk, the fading column of smoke from the crash site was still visible in the distance. The desert heat rose as the day went on and walking became even more difficult.

Robert started complaining every five minutes that he was thirsty, but Daniel kept a tight control on their supply of water. They didn't know how far they would have to walk to the next town, he argued. At this, Robert, who had become Daniel's biggest fan since the crash, started grumbling under his breath like he always did when he was about to go into a full sulk. Mum always ignored him when he got like that and Daniel seemed determined to do the same.

The sand of the desert had given way to a road of sorts, a firm dirt track that was about the width of a single car. It was easier on the feet than the shifting sand, but they made only slightly quicker progress. Overhead, there was no break in the ruddy, pendulous clouds.

They'd walked mainly in silence since leaving the plane, aside from Robert's complaining. None of them raised the issue of what they had seen again. Finally, Sarah could bear it no longer. Robert started to lag behind, so she took the opportunity to walk alongside Daniel.

"What do you think was going on back there?" she asked, a little breathless as they strode along. "You must have some idea."

All she received in response was a shrug.

"Hey, I want to know what you think!" she demanded, poking his arm.

"I'm as much in the dark as you are," Daniel replied, glancing round at her. "Maybe some kind of virus. Maybe something to do with the electromagnetism. Or maybe both."

"Perhaps it came to earth on the meteorite," Robert piped up, having quickened his pace so he could listen in to their conversation.

"And just what is 'it'?" asked Sarah.

"The sickness, of course," her brother replied as if she were being stupid. "The sleeping sickness might be from outer space. I saw on the telly that viruses can be carried on comets and meteors."

Even in the muggy heat, Sarah shivered a little.

"We don't know that," Daniel cut in, "so I don't see the point in speculating either way."

Robert's face fell.

"But it's a good idea, Bobbie," he added quickly, perking her brother up. Then he scratched his chin, as if thinking it over. "Perhaps they were all just pretending."

Robert laughed at this and said, "Yeah, maybe they were just being really lazy."

"Or sunbathing."

"Working on their tans."

Sarah laughed along despite herself, but stopped dead at a flash of light in the distance. A few seconds later a low rumble of thunder spread through the air. All three of them fell silent, looking in the direction of the lightning.

Another fork of lightning struck from the clouds and

hit the ground somewhere near the horizon. Again there was a gap of a few seconds before the thunder came.

"We should get moving," Daniel said, starting off again. "If it rains it's going to bring a lot of the dust down again. And there's nowhere to shelter out here."

Sarah thought of the storm that had caused the plane to crash and the sickness it had brought with it. She didn't want to be out in the rain.

"I'm tired," Robert moaned, dragging his feet. "We've been walking for ages. When are we going to stop?"

"When we find a town," Daniel replied, a new edge to his voice. He set off at twice the speed, not bothering to check if they were following. Clearly he didn't want to be caught in the rain either.

Sarah took Robert's hand and started pulling him along. He resisted, however, and sat down in the middle of the track.

"I want a rest," he said, folding his arms. Sarah was amazed at how he could change from laughing and happy to moody and sulky at the drop of a hat. He'd always been the same. She put her hands on her hips and prepared to give him a piece of her mind.

A shout from Daniel stopped her. He stood twenty metres up the road, pointing to a faded, hand-painted sign stuck in the ground. Sarah strained to see what it said.

Fresh milk, eggs, water. 2 km.

Pulling Robert to his feet, they set off with a new purpose. The air turned a little cooler as they walked, which was a relief, but also a reminder of the coming storm.

After another ten minutes they saw it in the distance: a single house by the side of the road. Sarah looked around at the empty landscape and wondered who would live in such a lonely place. The land certainly didn't look like it would be much good for farming, but then, what did she know?

"Is that a ute out front?" asked Daniel, straining his eyes to see. Sarah was momentarily confused, but understood what he was talking about when she made out the shape of a pick-up truck parked near the building.

With another ten minutes' walk they were getting close, despite Robert's renewed complaining and the rising wind, which was starting to whip dust around their faces again. Periodically, a severe gust of wind would almost knock them from their feet, but they struggled on.

"We're nearly there!" Sarah cried out as she shielded her eyes from another blast of dust-filled air. She tried not to think that it was probably the same dust that had carried the sleeping sickness to the survivors of the plane crash.

They reached a low fence that ran around the edge of the house and found a gate swinging open in the wind. Daniel led the way up to the front door of the wooden, single-storey building, stepping onto the long deck at the front. Only after he tried the handle of the door and found it locked did he bother to knock heavily with his fist.

"Nobody home," he shouted to them over the wind. "I'll try the back."

"Perhaps they're sleeping," Sarah called back, but got no response.

Daniel disappeared round the side of the building and Robert pressed his face into her arm to shield it from the wind. Something heavy started to drum on the iron roof of the house. The rain was finally coming.

It was then that Sarah had the strangest feeling – a kind of tingling up her spine and through her brain. She was suddenly certain that something was happening at the back of the house. Somehow she could see Daniel in her mind's eye and knew that he needed help. It was like nothing she'd experienced before.

"Come on," she said, dragging her brother round the side of the house to see if her instinct was right.

What she saw as they reached the rear of the building made her freeze and clutch Robert tighter.

A man stood in the open back door of the house. A towel was wrapped around his lower face as protection from the billowing sand. A short distance away, Daniel stood with his hands in the air.

The man had a shotgun aimed directly at Daniel's chest.

7

"Dad! Dad!"

Robert's shout made the man jerk the gun round in shock, but it was Daniel and Sarah who were the most surprised. Without warning, Robert slipped from Sarah's grasp and ran between Daniel and the gun.

"Robert!" Sarah cried above the sound of the wind.

"Stop pointing the gun at my dad!" he shouted at the man in the doorway, backing towards Daniel.

The man immediately lowered his weapon and pulled down the towel, revealing a bearded, sun-reddened face. He looked tired and confused.

"Is that your son?" the man demanded, waving the end of the shotgun in Robert's direction.

"Uh... yeah," Daniel said, as if getting used to the idea himself.

The man looked round at Sarah.

"My daughter," Daniel explained, placing a hand on Robert's shoulder. "We just want to shelter from the rain for a while. Please, for the kids."

Huge drops of rain were starting to splatter into the dirt all around them, creating muddy blotches all around. With a nod the man lowered the gun and led them quickly inside the house.

"Thanks," Sarah told the man as she joined Robert in the darkened kitchen. Looking around she saw four plates of half-eaten food laid out on the table, as if they had been abandoned mid-meal. The air had a musty smell to it.

The man leaned the gun against the door frame and motioned to the table. They sat as the rain hit. And what rain! It was as if a massive cauldron of water was being tipped out onto the house. Sarah looked through the window at the torrent pouring over the gutters and was thankful they weren't caught out in it.

"The name's Tom Barker," the man said, pulling the towel from around his neck and throwing it down on the floor. He slumped into a kitchen chair as if exhausted.

"I'm sorry about the gun," he continued. "I saw people coming and got worried. What with the bombs and everything."

Daniel looked at him in confusion. "The bombs?"

Barker nodded his head towards the window.

"The bombs in the desert," he explained. "There was the massive one that kicked up all the dust – we felt it. It almost shook the house down. Then we saw the explosion in the night. Who are we at war with?"

Daniel let out a little laugh and winked at Robert, who was sitting on his hands next to him.

"The big one wasn't a bomb, it was a meteorite. After that, you must have seen our plane come down. That's how we got here. Haven't you been watching the news?"

The man shook his head. "The TV's not working. Neither are the phones. Haven't been since last night. All the electricity's out."

"The EMP," Robert said and Daniel nodded.

Sarah looked around the room once more, her eyes falling on a series of pictures on the wall, photographs showing the man with his family: a woman and two teenagers. Daniel noticed them too and touched the edge of one of the dinner plates.

Barker must have guessed what they were thinking because he looked back to the door that led into the house.

"My family are sleeping," he said. "Otherwise you'd be able to meet my wife and kids. I'll see if I can get them up in a minute."

There was uncertainty in his tone. The rain hammered on the roof. There was a flash of lightning and a rumble of thunder seconds later.

"How long have they been sleeping?" Sarah asked.

"Since last night," Barker replied. "They just fell asleep at the table and now I can't wake them up. I can't..."

His voice cracked and Daniel stood. He laid a hand on Barker's shoulder.

"It's okay."

Daniel and Sarah found them laid out, still dressed, in each of their bedrooms. Barker must have carried them there from the kitchen. Sarah stood in the doorway of the son's bedroom while Daniel went inside and checked the boy's pulse. His face looked like he was in the most peaceful sleep imaginable, breathing deeply.

Daniel looked round at the door to check that he could still hear Barker, who was clearing plates in the kitchen in an attempt to keep busy, before putting his hands on the boy's shoulder and shaking him violently.

"Don't do that!" Sarah hissed, stepping into the room.

Daniel let the boy go and looked round, picking up a glass of water from the table next to the bed. Before Sarah could stop him, he threw the contents in the sleeper's face. The boy didn't flinch and certainly didn't stir.

"What are you thinking?" Sarah demanded, taking the glass from his hand and putting it back on the table. Daniel looked at her as if surprised by her annoyance.

"We have to find out. We have to find out how deep the sleep is."

"Well, how do you think the man with the gun will feel when he sees you throwing water on his son?" she whispered, taking a seat beside him. "What do you think it is?"

Daniel shrugged. "Seems to be some kind of coma. Perhaps virus related. I'm not a doctor."

"Are we safe being this close to him? I thought you said it's infectious."

"Yes, but I think we're too late to avoid exposure now," Daniel answered. "It only seems to affect some people, anyway. Remember the passengers who were still awake at the plane? Perhaps the three of us share some kind of immunity. Like a genetic inheritance."

Sarah laughed humourlessly. "I knew there would

have to be some benefit to being related to you, Daniel."

"Ha, ha."

Robert appeared in the door, hugging his arms across his chest.

"I don't like this house," he said. "That guy downstairs gives me the creeps."

"Keep your voice down if you don't want to be thrown out," Sarah whispered, pointing up at the roof and the incessant drumming of the rain.

"It's okay, Bobbie," Daniel said, getting up from the bed, "as soon as the rain stops we're out of here. Right?"

"Whatever you say," said Sarah.

Daniel smiled. "That was a brave thing you did, Bobbie. I think Mr. Barker's a little paranoid. I don't know what would have happened if I'd been alone."

Even in the dimness of the room, Sarah could see Robert blush with pride.

"But from now on we have to be more careful," Daniel continued. "Who knows who we'll run into on the road to Melbourne."

Robert looked at him quizzically. "What do you mean?"

Daniel leaned against the wall.

"There's been a disaster in this country. People can get kind of desperate. It's not nice, but it's true. At least that truck out front should speed up our progress. If it works, that is."

They fell silent for a moment. Sarah thought about the long road ahead before they reached the city. The sound of the rain battering the roof sounded more threatening than ever.

"What makes you think he's going to give us his truck?" Sarah asked finally.

"Oh, he's got to give it to us," Daniel replied, not looking round. "I think I'll be able to persuade him."

Sarah didn't ask any more questions.

The rain lasted for another hour and Barker said he hadn't known such a downpour in years. Daniel suggested it could bc something to do with the amount of dust that had settled in the atmosphere.

When it finally stopped they walked outside. The clouds still covered the sky above, but they seemed a lighter shade than before. The air had a strange metallic smell to it following the rain and the colours of the desert seemed brighter, more vivid.

While Barker was still in the house, Daniel led them to the utility truck and walked around it, inspecting the tyres and the interior through the dirt-smeared window.

He lifted the bonnet and looked over the engine, nodding slowly.

"It'll do," he said, pulling out the dipstick to check the oil. "Hopefully the engine wasn't knocked out completely by the pulse. Changing the battery water should do the trick."

Barker appeared in the doorway of the house and watched them at the vehicle, his arms folded.

"See anything you like?" he called, the harsh tone returning to his voice.

Sarah and Robert looked at one another. Daniel picked up his shoulder bag from the ground and started towards the building.

"Both of you stay here and don't move," he ordered.

Sarah began to follow him, but he looked round, his face deadly serious.

"For once, just do as I say," Daniel said before he turned and joined Barker in the doorway. They exchanged words and disappeared inside.

"What's going to happen?" Robert asked, looking after them.

"Why don't you check inside the truck?" Sarah said, trying the handle of the door and finding it unlocked. "See if there's anything we can use."

Robert was only too eager to start searching through the cab of the truck and was quickly engrossed. Sarah took the opportunity to run quickly to the house. She moved around the side to the kitchen window.

Peeping around the frame she saw Daniel and Barker in conversation at the table. Daniel said something and the other man stood, knocking over one of the chairs. She felt a sinking in the pit of her stomach, convinced that she was about to see something bad, remembering the gun.

What did happen was quite a surprise.

Daniel put his shoulder bag on the table and pulled out the silver glasses case she'd seen him fussing over just before the plane crashed. Unclipping a hidden panel on the bottom, he removed a small velvet bag and opened it. A glittering object dropped into his hand and he held it up for Barker to see.

A diamond.

Judging by the size of the bag, it wasn't the only one Daniel was carrying.

Keeping low, Sarah moved to the door, pressing her ear against the frame to hear anything she could.

"...enough to buy five more utes," Daniel was saying. "And your family will need medical help when all this is over. This can buy a lot of help."

"What about those kids?" Barker asked after a moment's thought. "Are they really yours?"

"They haven't been for a long time," Daniel replied, weighing the velvet bag in his hand. "But they are now. Look, I've got a delivery to make and I need that vehicle."

"What am I going to do with a diamond?"

"Here's the name and number of an associate in Melbourne," Daniel said, passing a scrap of paper across the table. "Call him when the phone gets fixed. He'll buy the item, no questions asked. Just don't take less than $50,000 for it."

There was silence, followed by the unmistakeable sound of a set of keys being thrown down on the table.

"Take it and go," Barker said.

Sarah hurried back round the house to the truck, trying to reach Robert first. He jumped out of the ute with a question in his eyes as she approached. Sarah raised a finger to her lips to silence him – she had to think. She knew one thing for sure: an engineer didn't carry around diamonds hidden in his flight bag. That was the kind of thing smugglers did. Was this why Daniel had left all those years ago? Had Mum thrown him out because he was a criminal, and if so, why hadn't she warned them?

From behind, Sarah heard the sound of the door opening again and Daniel's footsteps approaching. He carried Barker's shotgun in one hand and the set of keys in the other.

"Our carriage awaits," he said, jingling the keys at them. "Let's split this joint."

"Cool," said Robert. "I knew you'd do it! Can I carry your stuff, Daniel?"

Daniel raised a hand defensively to the bag on his shoulder and the secret it contained.

"That's okay, Bobbie," he said as he walked to the driver's side of the vehicle and tucked it under the seat. "I'll look after it. You take care of the backpack."

Robert shrugged and grabbed the bigger bag, throwing it into the open back of the truck.

"Mr. Barker was very nice and agreed to give us a box of food as well," Daniel said, nodding to the house. "Do you want to go and get it for us while I fix the battery?"

Robert didn't need to be asked twice, running back to the building. Alone, Daniel looked at Sarah carefully.

"Everything all right?"

She shifted her feet on the ground and looked at the road stretching away into the distance.

"Just looking forward to getting out of here," she said.

8

They found a map in the glovebox of the ute truck. Daniel spread it out on the dashboard as they drove a bumpy parallel track across the desert. The rain had passed and the landscape was now an endless sea of shifting red dunes as far as the eye could see.

"Looks like we landed somewhere in the Simpson Desert," Daniel said, pointing to a spot on the map whilst keeping an eye on the difficult track.

Robert sat between them, holding the map open, while Sarah examined the area across which they were travelling. She knew a little about the geography of Australia, having been made to study up by Mum. She could see that they were in the state called South Australia. The plane had gone down somewhere in the desert area and, if Daniel had his directions right, they were heading away from it towards the nearest settlement of any size: Innamincka.

"This way should take us right past the McKeever–Sikong oil refinery," Daniel explained, wiping the sweat from his forehead with the back of his hand. "We'll be able to get petrol there."

Sarah took another look at the map.

"Why aren't we heading to Adelaide?" she asked. "It looks closer than Melbourne."

Daniel shook his head.

"Melbourne's bigger and we'll pass through more places on the way," he explained. "Trust me. Besides, Adelaide was probably affected by the virus when the cloud passed over."

"I guess so," replied Sarah. Clearly Daniel's sights were set on Melbourne and he wasn't going to be persuaded against it. She kept quiet for a while and watched the dunes pass by, thinking all the time about the secret she had learned back at the house.

At least Daniel was a good driver. A couple of times

the truck almost lost control as it went over one of the ridges, but he always managed to keep it on track.

Having grown tired of looking at the map, Robert folded it up and put it down on the floor. He watched Daniel for a while.

"What's going to happen to them?" he asked eventually.

"Who?"

"Mr. Barker and his family," Robert explained.

"Oh, they'll be okay," Daniel replied casually. "They're just sleeping really. Mr. Barker is there to look after them."

"But how will they eat and drink? He can't feed them if they're asleep. What will happen? What will happen to everyone from the plane?"

Daniel fell silent, seemingly able to ignore the fact that Robert was going to stare at him until he got an answer.

"As soon as we reach a town we're going to send an ambulance to rescue them," Sarah said finally, realizing that it was up to her to reassure her brother. "They'll take Mr. Barker's family to hospital. They have ways to feed people who are sleeping. It's called intensive care."

Robert thought about this and nodded.

"Like Mum?"

Sarah's voice choked in her throat a little. "Yeah, like Mum."

Daniel glanced around at this, but made no comment.

They drove on through the desert until the dunes began to even out and the landscape became less sandy. The day was getting late and night started to fall quickly due to the dense clouds above. Daniel pulled the truck over by the side of the road and cut the engine.

"We'll stop here for the night," he said, rubbing his tired eyes. "It's too dangerous to keep on driving."

"Where will we sleep?" asked Robert.

"Where do you think, kid?"

"Under the stars?" Robert's voice was excited now. "Can we make a fire?"

"It wouldn't be camping without a fire." Daniel clapped him on the shoulder and jumped out of the truck.

They made their preparations for the night quickly. It was still warm, but a chill was coming to the air as the clouds finally started to roll away. By the time the sun had sunk in the west, a campfire was burning with the blankets laid around it, ready for them to bed down for the night. Sarah opened a tin of beans and some corned beef from the box Barker had given them. They set about making a simple meal.

Later, they lay back on their blankets and looked up at the night sky, visible now that the clouds were breaking up. Spreading out above them was an amazing vista of stars like Sarah had never seen. She'd lived in London most of her life, where at night the stars were all but lost in the ambient haze of the street lights. Out in the desert they shone brilliantly in the blackness, however. And not just one or two. Hundreds upon hundreds, packed together in clusters and constellations. It took her breath away.

"Wow," breathed Robert, who was lying on the other side of the fire.

"It's quite a sight, isn't it?" Daniel said from his own blanket. He'd removed the whisky bottle from his pocket and now took a swig. "At least this hasn't changed. Whatever goes on down here, the stars will shine on. See that constellation?"

They both looked to the area where he was pointing. A pattern of five stars stood out.

"The Southern Cross," Daniel said. "You can't see it from England. You have to be in the southern hemisphere, like Australia. That makes it special down here."

They watched for a while, enjoying the silence after the events of the day. Sarah heard Robert's breathing become heavier and across the flickering flames of the fire she saw that his eyes were closed. Getting up quietly, she placed another blanket over him.

"You're doing a good job looking after him." Daniel was watching her across the fire. She shrugged and settled back in her own place.

"Someone's got to," she replied, before realizing how it sounded. For once, she hadn't meant it as a dig. "Sorry."

"No worries," he replied. "I haven't been anyone's idea of Dad of the Year in the past. Eight years ago, when I left—"

"You didn't leave, Mum threw you out," Sarah corrected. "I'm not stupid, you know. I heard you two arguing all the time."

Through the flickering firelight, Sarah saw Daniel wince and take another drink. "Did she tell you why?" he asked.

"She never would. Want to let me in on the secret?"

"Another time maybe," he responded quietly. "So, she was still angry with me."

"Yes."

"And now you're angry with me too."

"I guess so."

"Your mum and I spoke, those last days at the

hospital," Daniel said. "She told me that you've been angry a lot recently."

Sarah fell silent. She remembered Mum's strained face, full of pain at another bad report from school. *Trouble.* That's what Sarah's last teacher had called her. That just made matters worse. In her last few months at school, Sarah had spent more time in the head-teacher's office than in class. After Mum became sick she just didn't like anyone telling her what to do.

"Everyone said she was going to get better," Sarah said finally, trying to control her voice. "All the doctors, the teachers. Even Mum."

"I'm sorry." Daniel took another drink from the bottle. His voice was starting to sound a little slurred...and sleepy.

"They lied to us," Sarah said, looking round at him, suddenly feeling angry. Angry at the plane crash and the meteorite. And angry at Daniel for lying too, keeping secrets. She almost challenged him about the diamonds, but stopped herself.

"All those months they knew she was going to die and they didn't tell us till the end," she said finally.

"Perhaps they were trying to protect you."

"Well, they shouldn't have," Sarah replied emphatically. "I'm sick of people keeping secrets. And I'm sick of lies.

From now on I'm not trusting anyone."

For a while they didn't speak. Daniel seemed to pick up on the fact that she didn't want to discuss it any more and fell silent, which she had to give him credit for. She listened to him take another gulp from the bottle.

A sudden thought occurred to her and she pushed herself up on her elbows.

"You don't think that it's happening all over the world, do you?" she asked. "The sickness, I mean. The virus?"

Daniel shrugged and began to answer, but stopped short as a light flared in the distance to the south-east. They both looked round to see a pillar of fire rising into the air, illuminating the clouds and desert around it.

"Is it another plane crash?" Sarah asked, standing to see better.

"I don't think so," replied Daniel, scratching his chin slowly. "It looks like a fire in the direction we're headed. The McKeever–Sikong refinery, most probably. One of the oil tanks must have exploded. What a mess!"

Sarah looked at the glow in the distance and shivered in the night chill. Suddenly everything in the world seemed more threatening than it had a day before.

"Get some sleep," Daniel said, wrapping the blanket around himself. "We've got a long way to go tomorrow."

Sarah lay down, but didn't close her eyes. She watched

as Daniel worked his way to the bottom of the whisky bottle and passed out. Then she waited until she could hear him snoring, worried that he might be pretending to sleep. Finally, taking care not to disturb either him or Robert, she pulled off her blanket and stood up.

Sarah crept to the truck, opened the door and felt under the seat for Daniel's bag. It took a minute of fumbling to find what she was looking for. Unclipping the false back of the case as she had seen Daniel do in Barker's kitchen, she removed the velvet bag. Drawing it open, she allowed three of the precious stones to drop into her palm. They shone in the light of the distant oil fire as she turned them over in her hand. Judging by the weight of the bag, it must have contained another twenty such diamonds at least.

Replacing the stones, she closed the bag and went through the situation in her mind. Finally she knew why Mum had thrown him out: Daniel was a criminal and had been on the run for the last eight years. He might have come back for them in their hour of need, but that didn't mean she trusted him. The only thing she knew for sure was that he needed to look after the diamonds.

And as long as she had them, he would have to look after her and Robert too.

9

Daniel muttered under his breath. His head was stuck in the engine of the truck as it had been for the last half-hour. On waking, they'd found clouds covering the sky again and the truck unable to start.

"I thought you said you were an engineer," Sarah said, watching him fumble with various parts of the engine without success.

"I build bridges, not cars," Daniel replied with a distinct edge to his voice. "Why don't you two go and play for fifteen minutes while I sort this?"

"But I want to help you!" Robert protested as Sarah dragged him away.

They wandered in the dunes for a while.

In the east, a column of smoke stretched across the horizon where the fire had been the night before. The flames of the fire weren't visible in the daylight, but judging by the amount of smoke, it looked as if it was still burning.

To keep Robert occupied, Sarah got him to collect rocks that looked interesting. That worked for all of two minutes before he started complaining he was bored. Normally Sarah would have just shouted at him, but she bit her tongue. She really didn't want to argue any more.

In the distance the sound of the truck engine firing sent them running back. They found Daniel standing by the open door to the vehicle.

"You fixed it!" Robert cried, running to the door. Daniel slammed it as he got close, drawing him up fast.

"What's wrong, Daniel?"

"Ask your sister," Daniel replied, his face dark and serious as he held up the shoulder bag in his right hand.

Robert looked round at Sarah, who managed a casual shrug.

"Lost something, Daniel?" she asked, meeting his gaze and holding it.

"I think you know what I've lost," he said, pulling the glasses case from the bag and tossing it at her feet. "I guess I should have kept a closer eye on my stuff."

Robert looked from Sarah to Daniel and back again in confusion.

"Sarah? What's he talking about?"

"He's not an engineer, Robert, just some kind of smuggler," she said, taking his arm and pulling him away.

"That's not true!" Robert cried, looking back at the man. "Tell her, Daniel."

"Sarah, it's not what you think," Daniel began, shaking his head. "I am an engineer. But sometimes I'm paid to transport things around the world as well."

Sarah let out a laugh.

"That's why you've got diamonds hidden in your flight bag, is it?"

"I need them back, Sarah," Daniel said evenly. "They don't belong to me and if I don't deliver them to Melbourne I'm going to be in serious trouble."

"And what if I don't want to go to Melbourne any more?" she said, standing firm. "What if I want to head to Adelaide? Or Sydney? Or the nearest police station?"

Daniel grimaced and reached through the open window of the truck, pulling out the keys.

"Then we'd have a problem," he said, taking a step towards them. "Why don't you just give back the diamonds, Sarah. We can carry on like nothing happened."

Robert turned on his sister. "You ruin everything!"

Sarah backed away in shock. "You don't understand, Robert..."

"Daniel saved us!" Robert's eyes were big and filling with tears. "Daniel helped us and you stole from him."

"He's the thief! How do we know we can trust him? He's lying to us, just like all the others!"

Without warning, Daniel stepped between them, his hand closing around Sarah's upper arm and squeezing. His eyes bore into hers and she felt her knees weaken as she tried to pull away.

"Where are they?" he demanded.

"Buried. In the desert."

"I don't believe you."

"I did it last night. While you were sleeping."

"You're lying."

"You're hurting me."

Daniel's grip tightened on her arm.

"I want that bag, Sarah."

They faced each other in silence for a moment, locked in a stand-off. Finally, the spell was broken as a small rock landed against the side of Daniel's head, causing him to turn in surprise.

"Let her go!" Robert cried out, picking up a more sizeable rock and hurling it at Daniel, who ducked to avoid it.

"Bobbie..."

"Let Sarah go! You're hurting her!"

Thinking fast, Sarah reached into the pocket of her jeans, pulling out the bag of diamonds. Robert saw what she'd done, so she tossed it through the air to him.

"Run!" she screamed as he caught it. Without needing to be told twice, her brother spun on his heels and started running for the dunes.

Daniel released his grip on her arm and started after him. Sarah followed, hot on his heels. For a minute they chased one another over the sand, Robert in the lead.

Finally, Sarah launched herself at Daniel's legs, bringing him down on the sand. The two of them rolled down the side of a dune together, struggling to be the first up. The truck keys slipped from Daniel's hand and Sarah snatched for them, beginning a scramble through the sand. Their fingers closed around the keys at the same time and their eyes met, each burning with determination. Remembering her karate, Sarah pulled back her hand to strike Daniel in the neck. One blow in the right place could fell the strongest opponent...

"Please stop."

The sound of Robert's voice, small and wavering, from a few metres away made them both freeze. They looked round to see him standing with his hand outstretched, offering the bag to Daniel.

"Whatever it is, you can have it back, Daniel," he said quietly. "I don't want us to fight."

There was a moment of silence as they looked at each other.

Finally, giving up his grip on the keys and breathing heavily, Daniel slumped back against the sand.

"I've made some mistakes in my time," he said, looking at them both. "But I never thought I'd end up having a fist-fight with my own kids."

"Welcome to being a dad," Sarah replied breathlessly as she lay back on the sand.

Unexpectedly, this sent Daniel into a fit. He threw his head back and laughed.

"Just give him the bag, Robert," Sarah said resignedly. "He wants it so badly."

Robert walked over with the bag. Daniel touched Robert's cheek with his hand, but didn't take it.

"I'm sorry I chased you, Bobbie," he said softly.

"Why don't you look after those for me until we get out of this?"

Robert said nothing, but ran to sit by his sister. Daniel nodded as the boy placed the bag of diamonds in his pocket.

"So, are you an engineer?" Robert asked.

"I was, once," Daniel said after a moment. "Then I got tempted by some...more lucrative lines of work. But when I heard your mum was sick, I promised I'd give that up. It was the only way she'd agree to let me back into your lives."

"It didn't take you too long to break that promise," Sarah said.

"You have to believe me, it was for us," Daniel protested. "I owe some serious people money and this was my way to pay them off for ever – get out of that life completely. It was to give us all a new start."

Sarah looked round at Robert and saw the tears in his eyes.

Daniel looked down at his feet. "I know I've messed up, but I'm your best bet for getting out of here. Unless you can drive a ute, that is. In Melbourne we'll talk about what we want to do. Whether you want me to be your dad or not. Until then, I promise I'll look after you the best I can."

Sarah squeezed her brother's arm as he wiped the tears from his eyes. She wanted to tell him that it was okay, that the guy wasn't worth it, but she knew it was no use. Sarah guessed it was just a hard lesson Robert had to learn. She looked round at Daniel, her face emotionless.

"Just get us out of here," Sarah said, refusing his hand as she pulled herself to her feet. "Go to the truck, Robert."

Robert ran to the ute without a word. Sarah and Daniel followed after, side by side.

"There, now you know I'm not going to ditch you both," he said. "Just make sure Bobbie doesn't lose that bag, or when we reach Melbourne I'll be the one getting dumped in the desert."

"Well, we wouldn't want that," she replied. "I guess."

There was really nothing else to say.

In the distance, unseen by any of them, something glinted amidst the dunes and then disappeared, like the sun reflecting off a pane of glass.

Or the lens of a pair of binoculars.

The man who had watched every move of their fight now tracked the truck as it sped away in the direction of the smoke column.

His hand reached for a walkie-talkie.

"Group Leader, this is Scout 3. Targets are mobile, heading south-east. Over."

The handset crackled back after a few seconds' delay.

"Good work. Intercept at the refinery. Over."

10

When they got within a couple of kilometres of the refinery, they saw fires burning out of control in at least two places, sending huge vines of black smoke trailing across the desert. The site was ablaze.

"A single spark can turn one of those oil storage tanks into an inferno," Daniel explained as they drew closer in the truck. They passed a towering billboard by the side of the road written half in English and half in Chinese. The title read *McKeever–Sikong Oil Refinery: the future of power, today!* Beneath the words, a Chinese and an

Australian worker shook hands.

"But where are the firemen?" asked Robert, talking for the first time since the incident in the desert. "Why isn't anyone trying to put it out?"

"I don't think the rescue services are anywhere near here, Bobbie," Daniel replied.

"And why exactly are we driving straight towards a fire?" Sarah asked.

Daniel tapped the fuel gauge of the truck. The needle pointed towards empty. "We won't get further than another twenty kilometres if we don't find some petrol. There must be a filling station for the tankers somewhere here. Hopefully not too close to those flames."

The iron gates to the refinery complex stood open. A guard's hut by the gate appeared deserted, but as they passed Sarah saw a man in a uniform slumped in a chair, another victim of the virus. Robert made a noise when he saw it, but Daniel shook his head.

"There's nothing we can do for him, Bobbie."

Ahead, the fire was raging, a monstrous, orange mass tearing through the oil tanks and the nearby buildings. The oil, stored there for processing, had ignited and was now feeding the fire without end. They stared at the terrifying sight for a moment through the dusty windscreen of the truck. The fire roared like a wild beast set free, making the windows vibrate.

"Have you ever seen anything like this before, Daniel?" Robert asked, straining to get a better view over the dashboard.

"Once," he replied softly. "Ten years ago in Iraq at an oil drilling platform. The only way they could stop the fire was to seal up the top with explosives. It took two days and four attempts before they managed to do it. We don't want to get too close to it, that's for sure."

Sarah pointed over to the left of the complex. There was a single storey building and a row of what looked like petrol pumps.

"Is that what we need?" she asked.

"Well, done, Sarah," Daniel said, putting his foot on the gas and driving the truck forward.

They followed a wide road past abandoned trucks and machinery, pulling up next to one of the petrol pumps. Daniel looked over at the open doorway of the building nearby.

"I'm going to fill up," he said. "Why don't you two check out the station? There might be stuff we need. See if you can find a petrol can we can fill."

Sarah looked at him with a raised eyebrow. He nodded and pulled the keys from the ignition.

"Trust me," he said, putting the keys in her hand. "Just don't stray too far. That fire can spread fast. We might need to get out of here in a hurry."

They jumped out and Daniel set to work with the pump. Sarah stuffed the heavy keys in her jeans and led Robert over to the building. The very air near the fire seemed hotter and she was aware of it growling in the distance.

Robert took her hand. "It's scary."

She gave his fingers a squeeze and smiled at him, trying to look reassuring. "We'll be quick."

The door to the building stood ajar and Sarah pushed it open cautiously with her free hand.

"Hello?" she called. "Anybody home?"

There was no response. She led Robert inside.

It was a storeroom of some kind. Boxes of crisps, chocolate bars and other snacks lined the walls, probably for the drivers who transported the processed oil from the refinery around the country. Robert's eyes widened as he saw a box filled with his favourite bar.

"Cool!" he said, grabbing the whole thing off the shelf, almost spilling the contents in the process.

"Great," said Sarah. "We get to live off junk food for the next week."

"So don't have any," Robert replied, his mouth already

half full with a bar. He picked up another and tossed it to his sister.

Shaking her head, Sarah opened the wrapper, finding herself suddenly starving. In the earlier excitement they'd completely forgotten breakfast. The chocolate inside was soft, almost melted in the heat, but it tasted better than any she'd ever had before. In a few bites it was gone.

"Another?" asked Robert, waving a second bar temptingly.

Mum wouldn't have approved, Sarah knew, but these were special circumstances. She nodded and they each started on a new bar, grinning at one another stupidly.

To the rear of the building something clattered, making them both start.

Sarah put her chocolate down on the nearest shelf and motioned for Robert to stay where he was. Walking quickly and quietly, she made her way past shelves and cardboard boxes, noticing a door in the far wall for the first time.

"Hello?" she called out. Her voice sounded small in the silence of the room. "Is someone there?"

Sarah reached out and tried the handle of the door, which turned stiffly.

The room beyond was small and dark, the only light

provided by a window set high up in the wall. In the middle of the room, an Asian woman was slumped over a desk, black hair spilling over a pile of paperwork. She clutched a ballpoint pen between her fingers as if she'd passed out in the middle of writing something. The scene gave Sarah a chill.

Something moved by the woman's feet and Sarah almost cried out. A ginger cat jumped forward and slid past her out of the door at full pelt.

"Just a cat, Robert!" Sarah called with relief as she backed out of the room. "Let's try to save it."

It was then that she experienced that strange feeling again: the one she'd felt on the front porch of the Barkers' house. Like a kind of warning light going off in her brain. Or a premonition of something bad.

Robert.

He wasn't standing where she'd left him. Her eyes darted to the door. A huge, white figure was dragging her brother away, its massive hand clamped over his mouth to stop him from crying out.

"Robert!" she cried out. The head of the thing turned sharply in her direction. Its face was an oval-shaped mirror in which she saw a distorted reflection of the storeroom and herself, small and stretched, standing in the doorway. For a moment all she could think was that an alien was taking her brother. A mirror-faced alien from the meteorite.

She followed without a second thought as they disappeared through the doorway.

Outside she saw Daniel by the truck, his arms held by two more of the aliens, which she now realized had to be men in suits, much like the ones she'd seen astronauts wear. The mirrored visors of their helmets made them look inhuman.

"Sarah!" Daniel yelled when he saw her. He struggled hard against his attackers. "Let me go!"

A third one stepped towards Daniel as he threatened to break their grip. There was something that looked like a can of deodorant in the figure's glove. The man sprayed the contents in Daniel's face and he immediately slumped back into the arms of his attackers, unconscious.

Sarah looked to her left and saw Robert being sprayed by another suit as he kicked against his own attacker. Within seconds he was lying still as well.

Fear took hold and she began to back away, feeling suddenly powerless against this new threat. After everything they had been through. What more could happen? The two suits holding Robert looked round at her.

She was next.

Sarah backed into something. Looking round, she found herself staring right into one of the mirror-masks, blocking her escape. In the helmet reflection, her eyes looked wide and fearful. She saw one of the cans raised, ready to spray in her face.

Sarah ducked forward and rolled between the legs of her attacker. The suited figure turned awkwardly and made a grab for her, but she was already running. Ahead, a wall of fire blazed. After a few metres she slowed to a halt. *Robert*, she thought. *Where am I going?*

Sarah turned slowly to see the three suited men approaching. One held what looked like a rifle in his arms. The suit raised the gun and took aim.

"No," whispered Sarah as the weapon was fired.

She staggered back as something hit her in the arm. Looking down, she saw a five-centimetre-long dart sticking into her flesh. She reached to pull it out as her knees buckled under her.

Then there was only blackness...

11

Sarah lay very still under cool, soft sheets. She stared at the white tiled ceiling for what seemed like a long time before trying to move. Her head ached and she wasn't sure how long she'd slept. It could have been less than an hour or a whole day.

Very slowly, she looked right and then left, taking in her new surroundings.

The room was a perfect square and completely empty apart from the bed in which she lay. Directly opposite the foot of the bed was a long mirror set into the wall.

Sarah's own image stared back. The reflection stimulated her last memory before she had passed out and she sat bolt upright. A jolt of pain shot through her skull and she raised a hand to her forehead reflexively.

"Headache?"

Sarah jumped a little at the unexpected sound of a woman's voice. It seemed to come from the mirror, but when she looked up she saw only her reflection. She was wearing a white smock, the kind Mum had worn in hospital. Sarah fingered the material nervously, bad memories coming to mind.

"Your clothes were filthy," the voice from the mirror explained. "They're being washed. Does your head hurt?"

"Yes," replied Sarah. She looked at the mirror and swung her legs out of bed. The tiles of the floor felt cool after the heat of the desert.

"Take this."

A panel opened in the wall to the right of the mirror. A tray slid out upon which a single glass of water and a small dish stood. Walking closer, Sarah saw that two pills lay on the dish. She poked them with her finger suspiciously.

"They're just aspirin," the woman reassured. Her tone was calm and soothing.

Her head was aching so badly, Sarah decided she'd just have to take the woman's word on that. She popped one pill after the other in her mouth, swallowing each with a gulp of deliciously cool water. She finished the rest of the glass and set it down on the tray.

"I bet you're starting to feel better already," the woman suggested.

Sure enough, Sarah could already feel the pain in her head subsiding. She peered at the glass, trying to see if she could make out anything behind it. She'd seen two-way mirrors in police dramas on TV and assumed there was someone watching on the other side.

"Who are you?" she asked her reflection, suddenly struck by the strangeness of it all.

"We're here to help," answered the voice. "My name's Mandy and I'll be looking after you from now on."

"Where's my brother? What's with all the mirrors?"

"We realize that you must be confused by the way you were brought in," Mandy replied, a note of regret in her tone, "but we needed to remove you from the hot zone as quickly as possible."

"Hot zone?" repeated Sarah. "You mean the fire at the refinery?"

The woman chuckled. "No. A hot zone is an area infected by a virus. From what your brother told us, we know you've seen the effects of the meteorite strike first hand. The survivors of the plane crash. The workers at the oil plant."

"Robert talked to you?"

"Why wouldn't he?" Mandy replied, as if the question confused her. "We're here to help."

Once again, Sarah started to feel the strange tingling sensation that had passed through her brain in the storeroom just before they were grabbed. This time, however, it was stronger, almost like the buzzing of the phone line connecting to the internet on her mum's ancient computer. She was filled with a very strong feeling that the woman behind the mirror was lying to her, hiding something. It was impossible to tell what it was, however, as the mirror seemed to be forming some kind of block. Sarah thought if only she could see the woman's eyes, she'd be able to tell more. Strange.

She also became aware that Robert was somewhere nearby, less than a hundred metres away. In fact, if she concentrated, she could almost...

Robert. Robert, are you there?

"Sarah, is everything okay? Sarah?"

The sound of the woman's voice snapped her back to reality and the strange feeling was lost. Sarah stepped away from the mirror, looking around the room. The sudden urge to smash the mirror grabbed her, to break down the thing blocking her odd, new instincts. If only there was a chair or something heavy…

"Sarah, someone is going to enter the room," Mandy broke into her thoughts.

"I want to see Robert."

"I don't want you to be afraid," the woman continued. "We're going to take you to your brother. Okay?"

Sarah nodded. One second later a section of the wall opened, revealing a door she hadn't noticed. Through it stepped one of the white-suited figures, the mirrored faceplate showing a fishbowl reflection of the room. Instinctively, Sarah backed away from the advancing figure.

"It's okay, Sarah!" Mandy exclaimed. "Delta-6, your mask!"

The suit stopped and reached up to press a button on the side of its helmet. Immediately the mirrored surface of the faceplate became clear glass, revealing the features of a man about the same age as Daniel. He smiled and beckoned her to follow him with a gloved hand.

"He won't hurt you," Mandy said. "Just go with him."

With a final look at the mirror, Sarah walked forward on slightly shaky legs. The suited man stepped aside so she could lead the way through the door.

Sarah moved into a corridor with curved walls and a flat floor. She brushed her fingers against the wall and found that it was made of a soft material that gave to the touch.

"Just keep walking," the man's voice crackled from a speaker in the suit. "That's right. Keep going to the airlock at the end. Don't stop."

When Sarah reached the circular hatch at the end of the corridor, the suited man swiped a card through a reader on the wall and it slid open. He gave her a little push with his hand to encourage her through.

Sarah stepped into a tube-like area that he'd called the airlock. A hatch clicked seamlessly into place behind her. There was a hiss of air and after a few seconds another, smaller, entrance opened before her.

"Step through," a voice commanded from hidden speakers.

Sarah climbed through the opening into a kind of plastic bubble. The hatch closed, sealing her inside the orb. Disoriented, Sarah leaned forward, pressing her hands against the clear plastic. As she did so, the bubble moved forwards and she slipped onto her hands and knees, almost rolling over as it went.

Carefully getting up, she looked round and saw a similar plastic bubble to her own standing a few metres away. Inside was Robert. He was dressed in a white smock like hers and had a big grin on his face.

Expertly, he moved his bubble towards her by walking forward and allowing the plastic sphere to turn around him as he went. Their bubbles touched and Sarah's bounced back a little, throwing her off balance. She fell and the bubble rolled with her.

Looking up, she saw Robert laughing and shook her head. He laughed even more at her efforts to get up again, sliding on her hands and knees. He started to run circles around her in his bubble.

"Robert, stay still a second!" she shouted at him, starting to get a little dizzy. "Robert!"

It was no use. No sound could pass out of the plastic capsule. Sarah looked daggers at her brother...

Stop that right now, Robert!

Robert stopped dead, staring at her. His lips moved, saying something that she couldn't hear. She tapped her ear and shook her head. Then he tapped his finger to his forehead and then pointed at her.

Somehow he'd heard what she thought.

Robert started mouthing something excitedly to her: do it again!

Sarah looked hard at him, concentrating...

Robert... Can you hear me?

He began nodding furiously, his mouth hanging open a little.

See if you can answer me...

He nodded and closed his eyes, frowning with concentration. A few seconds later he opened them again, looking at his sister expectantly. She shook her head and his shoulders slumped in disappointment. He looked at her and mouthed: how?

Sarah shrugged and shook her head.

I don't know...

She shot the last message across to him almost without thinking. It was getting to be just like talking. She thought of the strange feelings she'd been having since the plane crash and decided that it was probably part of the same change she was experiencing.

It's becoming easier, Robert... You have to keep on trying to answer... Something strange is going on here...

Any further experimentation with this odd new skill was stopped short as a door opened in the room and two men in white coats appeared. They looked like doctors or scientists, Sarah thought. One of them walked around their bubbles, plugging a little black box into a port on each. Speakers hidden somewhere in the structures crackled into life. The scientists left the room and were replaced by two men – soldiers, judging by their uniforms – who flanked the door.

Another figure entered: a tall man with crewcut, greying hair and piercing blue eyes. He wasn't wearing a spacesuit either, but a black military uniform. A radio microphone was clipped to his ear. When he spoke, his voice came through the speakers in the bubbles.

"Good morning," the man said, his accent clearly American. He cast a gaze over them with a smile. "My name is Colonel Randall Moss. I think it's about time we all got to know one another, don't you?"

12

"Where are we?" Sarah demanded, facing Colonel Moss. "Why have we been put in these things?"

"I'm sorry about the quarantine bubbles," he replied calmly, running a hand over his cropped hair. The colonel was in his mid-fifties, but clearly very strong under his perfectly pressed uniform. To Sarah he looked like a man who was used to getting what he wanted and his face showed the scars of someone who had been in his fair share of battles.

"You'll find that they're really the best way to get

around until we're sure you're no longer contagious," Colonel Moss continued. "I'm the local head of HIDRA and you're at our temporary base, six kilometres east of the refinery where we picked you up."

Sarah frowned. "HIDRA?"

"It stands for Hyper-Infectious Disease Response Agency," Colonel Moss answered, folding his arms and pacing in front of them. "We're an international task force designed to control ELEs. When a significant disaster occurs anywhere in the world, we step in."

"What's an ELE?" Robert asked.

"Extinction Level Event," Colonel Moss replied. "Outbreaks that threaten to destroy life on earth as we know it. I'm sure that you've worked out that the meteorite brought a virus with it. We call it the fall virus. It sends almost everyone who has contact into a kind of coma. Sometimes the effect is immediate, while others manage to hold out for a few days. The problem is, we don't have a treatment. Yet."

Robert and Sarah looked at one another through their bubbles, trying to take in all the information being thrown at them.

"You seem to know a lot about the virus already," Sarah said. "Were you expecting this?"

Colonel Moss looked at Sarah and nodded with a

smile, acknowledging her perceptiveness.

"You're right," he admitted. "It's not the first time it's happened. Two years ago a smaller meteorite hit South America with the same effects. The fall virus was devastating, but we managed to contain it to a few hundred kilometres in a sparsely populated area. Luckily."

"I never heard about that," Sarah said.

Colonel Moss nodded. "We worked hard to keep it secret. People just aren't ready to hear about a disease from outer space threatening the world. We think the meteorite that struck two days ago was from the same source. Maybe a planet that exploded. One that harboured the virus."

"Then there might be more meteors on the way," Robert said.

Colonel Moss nodded and they were silent for a moment.

"I don't see how that gives you the right to kidnap us..." Sarah began, but Moss cut her short with a wave of his hand.

"Firstly, you haven't been kidnapped, you've been rescued," he said, beckoning a soldier at the door over. "Secondly, we should be the ones asking questions."

The soldier approached, holding up the bag of diamonds in his fist.

"What's that?" Sarah asked.

"Please, don't play games," Colonel Moss replied. "We found over two million US dollars' worth of diamonds in your brother's pocket. I'm assuming your father gave them to you, thinking a child wouldn't be searched."

Sarah and Robert exchanged a glance. Colonel Moss snapped his fingers and one of the soldiers approached with a laptop computer. He held it up for them to see. The screen showed an official record marked *INTERPOL Datasheet*. Daniel's picture was in the top right corner next to a list of crimes: smuggling and forgery among them. "I'm sorry to be the one telling you this, but your father is wanted in several countries. Looking at the record of your flight, this is the first time he's travelled under his real name in nine years. He was taking quite a risk."

"He came back for us," Robert said softly.

Colonel Moss snapped the laptop shut and the soldier took it away. "We think he wanted a cover to bring the diamonds into Australia. That's why your father was travelling with you. No doubt his buyers are criminals looking to sell to rich Australian clients.

"The truck you were driving belonged to the owner of the farmhouse where we found another diamond," he added. "Tom Barker and his family are now in intensive care."

"Mr. Barker got sick too?" Sarah asked.

"Adults who come in contact with the virus always get sick," Colonel Moss replied. "Most children do too."

"Apart from us," Sarah said. "And Daniel."

"That's not correct, Sarah," Moss said with a shake of his head. "Your father's blood test came back positive. He went into a fall virus coma two hours after we picked you up."

"That's not true!" With a cry of anger, Robert rushed at Moss, the bubble rolling with him. The colonel caught the surface of the sphere with both hands and held him fast. Inside, Robert collided with the plastic and fell back with a cry…

Daniel! Sarah, Sarah!

Robert's words split Sarah's brain like a bolt of lightning, but he hadn't spoken aloud. She saw Robert staring at her, his eyes wide and tear-filled. His mental block was broken, Sarah realized. She held up a hand as if to stop his thoughts.

Robert, slow down! You're hurting me!

Robert's mouth fell open as he realized that his sister was receiving him. She made a warning motion with her hand.

Keep it to yourself! Don't let him know!

Something, perhaps that strange instinct she was developing, told her that they should keep their new ability secret until they knew more about it themselves.

"I'm sorry, Robert," Colonel Moss said sympathetically. "It's the truth. I wish I had better news for you."

"He was fine..." Robert struggled to his feet and manoeuvred his bubble over to Sarah.

Moss gave a sigh. "I've seen it all before, son. Daniel held out longer against the virus than most, probably because he shares the same genetic make-up that gives you two your immunity."

"But why him and not us?" Robert persisted.

"In adults the disease is devastating," Colonel Moss went on. "At the moment you're both what we call *carriers* – immune to the disease but able to pass it on to others. Our experience with the virus so far suggests you'll remain infectious for another seventy-eight hours at least. Until then, you'll be kept in strict quarantine."

The colonel allowed that information to sink in for a moment before adding, "I promise your dad's getting the best medical attention possible. Nobody knows more about the fall virus than my people."

Sarah bumped her bubble against Robert's to get his attention.

It's okay, Robert. He's right. Daniel's in the best place.

It seemed to calm her brother a little. Sarah just hoped it was the truth. She turned away from Robert and met the colonel's eyes. They were a beautiful blue, but there was a coldness at the centre. She tried to read him, like she had the woman behind the mirror, to find out what he was really thinking. Perhaps her new intuition wasn't so strong after all, however, because he was a complete blank.

"Are you feeling okay?" the colonel asked, taking a step towards her. She realized that she'd been staring at him and looked away. "I understand how difficult this is for you. Robert told us about losing your mum… How Daniel hasn't really been much of a father to you. I want you to know that HIDRA will take care of you both."

"We want to see Daniel," Sarah said, trying to sound stronger than she felt. "We barely know him, but he helped us. He was the one who saved us from the plane crash."

"He's still in a very unstable condition," Colonel Moss replied. "No one other than our doctors can enter the intensive care zone. He'll be kept at that status for several days, I'm afraid."

Sarah and Robert exchanged a look. Moss seemed to sense their disappointment.

"In the meantime, let me show you some of the open access areas of the base," he said. "So you can see the kind of treatment Daniel will be getting."

He turned and strode across the room to the door. With the swipe of a security card, it opened. Sarah and Robert waited hesitantly.

"Well, come on!" Colonel Moss said, gesturing towards the door. "It's perfectly safe."

13

As Sarah manoeuvred her bubble out of the building, she expected to see the desert outside. However, she found herself standing in a huge enclosed space, the size of ten football pitches at least. Moving carefully inside the bubble, Sarah walked down a ramp from the door, followed closely by Robert. At the bottom of the ramp they both stopped and took in their new surroundings.

Looking up, Sarah did not see the dust-filled sky, but rather a massive, domed ceiling. The floor was covered in a kind of dark plastic, the same material as the dome. Glancing around, she took in more than twenty long, white buildings. They seemed makeshift, little more than big mobile homes, as if designed to be put up and taken down in a hurry. In one corner stood a row of military trucks and jeeps. There was even a helicopter, a sleek, black thing on a trailer with its blades folded up.

A formation of soldiers in sandy-coloured HIDRA uniforms marched by. They turned their heads as one and saluted as they passed. Sarah was taken aback, but then noticed Colonel Moss had appeared at her side. He returned the salute briskly and watched the troops as they continued on their way.

"Wow," Robert said as he reached the bottom of the ramp. "Is this all yours?"

"This is all HIDRA's," Colonel Moss explained. He caught sight of Sarah looking up and pointed at the ceiling. "We can put the dome up in less than an hour. It's quite a feat of engineering, completely secure. The material is a polymer we created ourselves in the labs – extremely strong. Right now it's keeping us safe and allowing my people to go about their work in the hot zone without having to wear protection suits all the time. As soon as we know for sure you're not carrying the virus, we'll get you out of those bubbles."

“What about when you want to go outside?” Robert asked, ever-inquisitive.

Moss gestured to the far side of the dome. A tunnel the size of a house was set into the outer wall. The entrance was blocked by two massive iron doors and surrounded by a squad of armed soldiers.

“That’s the airlock,” the colonel explained. “Any personnel or vehicles leaving the dome have to pass through there and undergo a fifteen-minute sterilization process. It keeps the virus out. And don’t worry: it’s absolutely the only way into the dome.”

Sarah looked at the soldiers guarding the airlock. They wore a black and gold uniform different to the others. She wondered if they were some kind of special group – they looked serious, even more so than the normal soldiers.

“And it’s the only way out,” she added.

Colonel Moss shrugged. “I guess you could say that. Come on.”

They followed him in the direction of one of the other buildings. Sarah was starting to find walking in the bubble easier, although she was aware how stupid she must look: like she was in some kind of oversized snow-globe. They passed several soldiers and white-coated scientists on the way, but none gave them as much as a second look. Sarah guessed that seeing people walking around in giant, inflated bubbles was pretty normal at HIDRA.

They reached a building marked *Sleeper Modules B*. A ramp led up to the entrance, making it easy enough for Sarah and Robert to traverse. Colonel Moss led the way and they followed passively.

The door opened into a single room filled with rows of what looked like sarcophagi from an Egyptian tomb. Each of these, however, was plain white with a glass screen set into the top. As the colonel led them along one of the rows, Sarah saw that each sarcophagus was filled with a sleeper. She stopped next to one that she recognized from the plane: Nicole, the flight attendant. Through the screen, Sarah made out sensors attached to the woman's body, while a computer read-out on the side of the casket kept track of her heart-rate and other vital information.

Robert asked, "Are they all—"

"Victims of the virus," Colonel Moss finished for him. "Many of these come from your plane crash. The caskets keep their condition stable and provide everything the sleepers need – food, water and waste disposal. But of course, this is just a fraction of the total number affected."

"You mean there's more than this?" Sarah asked,

looking around the room. There had to be at least four hundred sarcophagi packed inside.

The colonel stopped by one of the caskets and looked at her.

"You and Robert have been incredibly lucky," he said. "We've got four rooms like this filled already. We're trying to control the spread, but more importantly we need to find a cure fast – before the virus reaches one of the major cities. If it does, we'll be dealing with millions of people, not thousands."

Sarah sensed he was building up to something. She decided to ask first. "What do you want from us?"

Colonel Moss smiled, approving of her directness. "We need your help. You and Robert are special, immune to the fall virus. Maybe you contain a cure for all this. We can stop more suffering and maybe we can bring Daniel and all the others back. We need to do tests... I can't promise that it will be easy..."

Sarah looked at Colonel Moss. Once more, she found him impossible to read. However, she knew they had a responsibility to help in any way they could. She'd work out the colonel and HIDRA later.

"We'll help any way we can. Right, Robert?"

Her brother looked round from the casket. She saw tears glistening in his eyes.

"For Daniel," he said, voice barely above a whisper.

The colonel smiled approvingly. "You're doing a very brave thing. I just want you to promise me one thing: tell us about anything strange that happens to you. The virus can have...unpredictable effects. Any information could be useful – anything at all. No matter how trivial it seems. Okay?"

Sarah met his eyes and nodded. But once again, her instincts told her that revealing everything to the man before they knew what was really going on would be a mistake. She had the feeling Colonel Moss wasn't telling her the whole truth.

"Sure," she said. "We'll let you know everything, but I can't think of anything unusual at the moment."

Colonel Moss nodded and gestured to the soldiers waiting at the door. "My men will take you back to your rooms."

A few minutes later, Colonel Moss strode from the casket room to another building. Two black-and-gold-uniformed Special Forces soldiers guarded the entrance. The colonel saluted his elite soldiers and carried on into the building.

Inside, he entered a smaller room in which a two-way

mirror looked into an adjoining cell. At a metal table inside the cell sat Daniel Williams. There was a bruise forming around his eye and his lower lip was split, but his face was defiant.

By the window, Colonel Moss's second-in-command, Major Bright, looked round. Although he was almost twenty years younger, Major Bright was an identical make of soldier to the colonel: hard, experienced and determined to achieve his goal at any cost. One of his most striking characteristics was a scar that ran down the side of his face from his right ear to the tip of his chin. Colonel Moss was one of the few people at HIDRA who knew how Major Bright got the scar. The rest were just too afraid to ask.

"Did the children buy the story, Colonel?" he asked.

Colonel Moss nodded. "I told them their father went into a coma – they had no reason to disbelieve me. What happened to his face?"

"He didn't take kindly to some of our questions, sir," Major Bright said, eyes flashing. He ran his forefinger along the groove of his facial scar, as was his habit from time to time. "He's strong, this one."

"Like his daughter," Colonel Moss replied, showing no sign of disapproval at the injuries inflicted. "The girl claims to have experienced no side effects so far."

"Do you believe her, sir?" the major asked. "Perhaps they haven't started developing like the others. We have more persuasive methods to bring on the change than the scientist-run tests..."

"Patience, Major," Colonel Moss answered, smiling at his second-in-command's eagerness. Bright was aggressive, a trait that Moss found useful sometimes but which needed close supervision. "You'll get your chance with them. For now, we'll use kid gloves. Dr. Andersen is already asking too many questions about the special abilities programme."

Major Bright nodded and indicated Daniel. "What about him, sir? He's demanding to see the children."

Colonel Moss scratched the stubble forming on his chin. "I was hoping the virus would've taken hold by now, but he seems unusually resilient."

"Keeping their father around is an unnecessary complication," Major Bright said, moving closer to his superior. "We can't hide him here for ever without the scientists on the base getting wind of something. It might be days before the virus kicks in."

Colonel Moss nodded. "He could get in the way of our plans for the children."

On the other side of the glass, Daniel looked directly at Moss. Again there was that defiance.

"Just give the word, sir," Major Bright said quietly.

Colonel Moss considered a moment before finally deciding, "Let's *relocate* Daniel Williams. I take it you can select the best men for the job?"

"The Special Forces team is loyal only to you, Colonel."

Moss nodded. "Drug and hide him in one of the sleeper caskets for now. Then I want him dumped in the desert. Dehydration will do the job if the virus doesn't first. And put the diamonds on him – I don't want anything tying back to us."

"And the children..."

"Will give us what we want eventually, just like the others," Colonel Moss replied coldly. "Thirty years of soldiering has taught me one thing...orphans make the best recruits."

14

The tests began the next afternoon. Or at least, Sarah assumed it was afternoon. She found it almost impossible to measure the passage of time accurately in her windowless room. When the scientists wanted her to sleep they dimmed the lights. When they wanted her awake they raised them again.

Food was bland meat and vegetables brought in on metal trays three times a day. Most of the time, she wasn't hungry enough to eat more than a few mouthfuls of these boring concoctions. The pills they gave her made her feel sick whenever she ate, anyway. She was given a stack of magazines and books to keep her occupied, but no music or television. Mandy encouraged her to keep a diary in a ruled exercise book brought by one of the suited men. Despite the flood of thoughts rushing through her brain, Sarah only wrote a few lines. The feeling that she should keep her new powers a secret for as long as possible hadn't gone away. HIDRA just wanted a cure, didn't they? She'd tell them about her new ability when she knew what was going on herself.

At regular intervals, men or women in protective suits entered to take blood samples or run various tests. Sometimes they got her to exercise while they monitored her heart-rate. Sometimes sensors were attached to her head that she had to wear while she slept.

Other tests were stranger.

On one occasion Sarah was taken to another room, identical to her own, except without a bed. She was left alone for ten minutes before the sound began. It started as a low hum, barely noticeable, and grew in intensity until it was an annoying ringing in her ears. Sarah shouted at the mirror, where the noise seemed to be coming from, but there was no response. The sound grew...and grew...and grew...

Until it seemed to be splitting her skull.

Finally, she'd curled up in the corner, trying to block the noise with her hands over her ears. At some point she passed out…

Sarah awoke some time later in her own room again.

"What happened?" she asked the mirror as aspirin and water were provided through the slot in the wall.

"I know some of our procedures are difficult to understand, Sarah," Mandy's voice in the mirror reassured. "But you said you'd help us. Thousands and maybe millions of people can be saved by the tests we're carrying out."

"I don't understand how…"

The reply was curt. "Sarah, we're scientists. Trust us."

"I want to see Robert. And I want to speak to Colonel Moss."

"That's not possible right now. Please, Sarah. Be patient."

So she was. For the time being.

Sarah could sense Robert close by and the feeling got stronger hour by hour. Often she would lie on the bed and close her eyes, focusing on the part of her mind where she could sense his presence. His room was only a hundred metres away, she could tell. Concentrating harder, she began to pick up his emotions: happiness, boredom, anger, fear. Very occasionally a thought of his would snap into her brain, like a voice shouting in her head, before it disappeared again.

She couldn't fully control the power yet, but it was coming.

Again and again in her sleep she dreamed of Robert speaking to her and woke up shouting an answer to him.

"Is everything okay?" Mandy would ask from the other side of the mirror.

"Just a bad dream," Sarah answered, turning over in the bed.

Sometimes she'd cry in the night, thinking about how she would have given anything to see Mum again for just a few seconds. Mum would've known what to do and would have been strong for both her and Robert. Very much to her surprise, she also found herself wishing that Daniel was there – but he was gone too, lost to the virus. Sarah knew that she was the one who was going to have to be strong for her brother now. She buried her tears in the pillow.

She wouldn't let them see her cry.

* * *

"How much further?" the Special Forces soldier in the driver's seat of the truck grumbled as it bumped along the desert track.

Beside him, his commander tapped the odometer and replied, "Another couple of klicks."

Major Bright had been precise with his instructions: the prisoner was to be dropped in the desert one hundred kilometres to the west of the base – no more, no less. Right now he was lying sedated in a sleeper casket in the back of the truck.

A few moments later, the commander signalled for the truck to stop at the top of a dune.

"Okay, helmet on," he ordered and both men fitted on their mirror-masks before moving into the back of the cab. They stepped into the airlock and closed the hatch. The cab of the truck was completely sealed and took in air from the outside only once it was thoroughly filtered. The air outside was still contaminated with the airborne virus and would be for at least three more days according to the HIDRA scientists.

Checking the internal door was thoroughly sealed, they opened the external door and stepped out into the forty-five degree heat of the desert. Their combat-model HAZMAT suits were fitted with cooling units, but they could still feel the intense sun beating down.

"Let's get this over with quick," the commander said as they walked to the back of the truck. He pulled down the back door and they both grabbed the end of the sleeper casket, hauling it out. The unit slipped unexpectedly from their gloved hands, rolling down the side of the dune all the way to the bottom.

"Ouch, that's gotta hurt," the younger soldier said, thinking of the drugged prisoner inside the casket.

The commander shook his head. "Well, we're the ones who have to drag the casket back up to the truck. Major Bright said leave no evidence."

The other man groaned and they started down the dune, kicking up arcs of sand as they went. "Just what did this guy do to get on the wrong side of Major Bright so bad?"

"Maybe he asked too many questions," the commander said pointedly as they reached the casket. He pulled a lightweight dart-gun from his belt, as did his companion. They'd been ordered to use non-lethal force to avoid suspicions being aroused if the body was ever found.

The commander grabbed the release handle of the casket and threw it open. What they saw inside made them both step back...

It was empty.

The commander crouched by the casket and examined

the interior. There were signs of damage to the frame, as if someone had been kicking at the lid from the inside. Clearly, the prisoner hadn't been given enough sedative to last the journey. Which led to the question, where was he now?

Both soldiers looked back up the dune to the open back of the truck and then at one another.

"Okay, let's take it slowly," the commander said.

The other soldier nodded and they started back up the dune, dart-guns raised...

They spotted him crouching near the back of the cab – no doubt trying to get in through the airlock. They'd been sure to lock the door, of course. Sensing their approach, the prisoner made a break for it, running wildly into the dunes. The young soldier raised his dart-gun, but the commander placed a hand on his arm.

"Don't waste your darts," he said, watching the prisoner fleeing into the distance. "There's nowhere for him to go – he'll die out here within a day."

The other soldier lowered his gun and nodded, a little disappointed to miss the chance to shoot someone.

"All right, let's get the casket and get back to the base," the commander ordered. "I'm starving."

Five minutes later they had the evidence of their presence back in the truck. The prisoner was nowhere to be seen, so they went back through the airlock. Job done – they both agreed there was no need to tell Major Bright the details of how the prisoner had escaped…

Hidden amid the dunes, Daniel watched the truck circle round and depart in the direction from which it had come. As it disappeared into the distance, he stood up and dropped the air filtration unit he'd removed from the back of the cab onto the sand. If his understanding of the cab system was correct from his quick analysis, the soldiers in the truck were now breathing unfiltered desert air – completely virus-contaminated.

Daniel started to follow the tracks of the truck back towards the HIDRA base. The sun began to beat down feverishly on his back and his mouth already felt parched. He hadn't had a drink in what seemed like days and now he faced the prospect of a walk through the desert. Daniel knew it wouldn't be long before his body gave up to the effects of dehydration.

He just hoped that the soldiers succumbed to the virus and that he found the truck before then...

Inside the dome, Major Bright knocked briskly on the door of his superior's office. Colonel Moss looked up from a stack of paperwork, his face dark.

"Problem, sir?" Major Bright asked.

Moss held up one of the papers – a printout of a lengthy email. "Sent by our chief scientist to General Wellman. She doesn't know anything about our real plans yet, but she's a potential problem."

"I'll keep an eye on her, sir," Major Bright replied.

"Very good." The colonel put the printout in his desk and slammed the drawer shut.

"The matter in the desert has been taken care of," Major Bright continued. "Our men just radioed it through. We're ready to proceed."

Colonel Moss smiled coldly. "Excellent. Have you briefed the men?"

Major Bright nodded. "Special Forces have been informed we're stepping up the programme, sir. They're ready to institute a full lockdown of the base if necessary. But I don't anticipate problems: these scientists have no stomach for a fight."

"Good work, Major," Colonel Moss replied. "It's time we got some real results. Prep the tank for the experiment. I want Sarah Williams to be the first test subject. Project Superhuman is a go."

15

Robert screamed.

Sarah! Sarah! Help!

She'd been dozing, half asleep although the lights were fully up. They'd taken almost a pint of blood earlier and given her some new pill. It made her feel so tired, she could barely keep her eyes open. She'd been having the strangest dream – something about Daniel and an endless desert. They'd been running through the sand together, desperately looking for something they'd lost...

Sarah!

Robert's voice rang through her brain as clearly as if he was in the same room. She almost fell out of bed.

Robert, it's okay! she sent back. *Can you hear me? What's happening?*

There was no response.

Sarah ran to the mirror and placed her hands on the glass.

"Is there anything wrong, Sarah?" Mandy asked. Something in her voice suggested she'd been expecting some kind of reaction from Sarah right at that moment.

"I want to see Robert," Sarah demanded. "He needs me!"

"And what makes you say that?" Mandy asked, a note of triumph in her voice, as if she had backed Sarah into some kind of corner. "Is there something you want to tell us?"

Sarah lowered her hands and stepped away from the mirror. Her instinct cried out in her mind once more: that she should keep it a secret from Mandy. But now Robert needed her. Sarah stood motionless, torn between keeping her secret and revealing all in the hope it would get her to see her brother sooner. In the end, it was decided for her.

The door beside her slid open without warning. A stranger stepped into the room. He wore a protective suit and helmet, although one bearing the black and gold of the Special Forces. Sarah judged that he was in his mid-thirties – there was a hardness to his face that she immediately disliked. A nameplate on the chest read *Major Bright.*

"You promised to tell us everything, Sarah," he said, fixing her with piercing eyes as she shrank back on the bed. "But I don't think you've been one hundred per cent honest with us, and neither has your brother."

"What are you talking about?" Sarah cried out as a soldier in a similar uniform and mask stepped into the room.

"Take her to the tank," Major Bright commanded.

The soldier grabbed her arm roughly and dragged her towards the exit.

Moments later she was in a bubble and being half led, half pushed towards a building she'd never been inside before. It was larger than the others and stood slightly apart from the rest. Two armed guards on the door stepped aside as they approached. Sarah stumbled on the bottom of the ramp, but one of the suits gave the bubble a push, rolling her forwards in the most undignified way possible. She cried out in protest, but the suit gave no sign of having heard.

Then she was inside the building.

Sarah struggled to her feet in the bubble as a door was closed behind her. She stood at the edge of a tank of water the size of a swimming pool. On the opposite side, two suited soldiers stared back at her in silence. They carried dart-rifles like they'd used at the refinery. Sarah moved the bubble to the edge and looked down at the water's surface, half a metre below. The tank looked as if it was at least four metres deep, the water still but threatening.

Somebody approached from behind. She looked round to see Major Bright standing close to her bubble and flinched away. Up close, he was one of the most imposing people Sarah had ever met. Her eyes were uncontrollably drawn to the long scar running along the right side of his face. It made him look dangerous. Colonel Moss might pretend to be friendly, but this man could never get away with it. Major Bright grinned, as if sensing her fear and repulsion.

"Okay, Sarah," he said. "Let's see what you can really do."

He placed a gloved hand on the bubble and pushed. With a cry, Sarah fell back into the tank, powerless to resist.

For a moment she floundered helplessly as the bubble rolled around on the surface of the water. At the edge of the tank, Major Bright held up an object that looked like a TV remote. He pressed a button and immediately the bubble collapsed around Sarah, like a balloon that had been pricked with a pin. The torn material clung to her like a wet plastic bag.

Sarah sank to the bottom of the tank like a stone.

16

Somewhere in the back of Sarah's mind, an instinct or maybe a memory of the life-saving class she'd taken at the local pool back home kicked into gear.

When she touched the bottom of the tank, rather than struggle and thrash against the ripped plastic weighing her down, she calmly pulled it away from her face and shoulders. With all her strength, she pushed her body out of the layers of plastic and kicked upward. Sarah broke the surface of the water a few seconds later and gulped in a mouthful of air.

Looking around wildly, she saw the tall figures of the soldiers and Major Bright walking around the side of the tank. A whirring sound filled the air and she turned, trying to make out where the noise was coming from. *They were trying to kill her!* She fought down that wave of panic and began to swim for the edge of the water, aware of something moving across the top of the tank.

"Try to stay focused, Sarah!" Major Bright called to her from the other side. "I think you'll find this a very interesting experience."

Sarah ignored the voice, swimming hard for the other side. If she could just get out before they pushed her back in…

Something was sliding across the top of the tank. Sarah stopped swimming and looked up to see a surface like a massive glass window pass above her head. On the other side she could see another surface sliding out. Seconds later, the two met in the middle of the tank with a *clunk*, forming a lid over the water.

Sarah reached up, placed her hands on the glass and looked around. There was about half a metre of air between the water and the lid, with no visible way out at the edge of the tank. She started to feel the claustrophobia of being trapped between the water and the glass, gasping for breath uncontrollably. Sarah closed her eyes and centred herself. The tank was huge. There was enough air to last for hours.

Footsteps approached across the lid.

Sarah opened her eyes to see Major Bright standing above her. Clearly it was strong enough to hold his weight, so fat chance of breaking through. Major Bright looked at her floating below him, like he was studying a bug under glass.

"Sarah, can you hear me?" His voice was piped into the tank through speakers at the edge.

She nodded up at him, powerless to do anything else.

"We're going to try a different test today," Major Bright continued. "The tank is going to fill with more water. I want you to try to get out before you drown. Okay?"

Sarah stared up at the man in disbelief. He delivered this last piece of information like he was asking if she fancied a diet cola. She slammed her palm against the glass and screamed at him. Above her, he tapped the side of his helmet and shrugged to show that he couldn't hear.

"Try to save your breath, Sarah," Major Bright said as he turned and walked back towards the edge. "I'm sure you'll surprise us all..."

On either side of the tank, the sound of water churning

grew, like taps running into a bath. Sarah wheeled around, aware that the gap between the surface of the water and the glass was getting rapidly smaller. In less than a minute, it was down to thirty centimetres. In desperation, she half-swam, half-pulled her way along in pursuit of the man above her.

"Help me!" she cried, despite the fact she knew her persecutors couldn't hear. "You can't do this!"

But they could do it. And they were.

The water went over Sarah's mouth and nose briefly and she panicked, going under the surface. When she kicked back towards the lid she found that there was less than ten centimetres of air – and that was disappearing fast. Tipping her head back, Sarah took one last, desperate intake of breath and filled her lungs as the tank topped up completely with water.

For a moment Sarah hung there, suspended one metre beneath the glass. There was nowhere to run. No air left. Only water. And death.

With a powerful frog kick, she sent herself gliding through water towards the feet of one of the soldiers standing on the glass. Turning in the water, she kicked her feet desperately at the glass ceiling to attract his attention. The soldier looked down – their eyes met...

HELP ME! she screamed out in her head.

Behind his mask, the soldier's eyes widened. A jumble of confused images tumbled through her mind: soldiers marching in parade, a plane crashing, Colonel Moss and (most disconcertingly) herself floating in the tank, viewed from above. Sarah came to a sudden realization: *the images were from the soldier's mind!* Somehow, she was accessing them directly. The air in her lungs began to burn like fire and she released it in a cloud of bubbles. With all her strength Sarah kicked the glass again, realizing that she only had seconds left before she started drowning.

DO SOMETHING! BREAK THE GLASS! SHOOT IT!

She repeated the orders like a chant in her mind...

The soldier held her eyes, dropping the dart-rifle to his feet. Not breaking her gaze for a second he reached to his belt and extracted a hand pistol. He aimed it directly between his boots, finger on the trigger. Sarah stared down the barrel, aware that he was about to fire blindly in her direction. In desperation, she arched round and away from the path of fire.

A muffled explosion vibrated through the water...

Sarah looked round in time to see the path of the bullet as it pierced the glass and carried on down to the bottom of the tank, leaving a trail of bubbles in its wake. A split second later, the section upon which the soldier was standing shattered. He plunged into the water, surrounded by a thousand shards of glass.

Not waiting another second, Sarah pushed towards the gap in the lid, swimming through the glass fragments as best she could. Her lungs screamed out for air. She broke the surface and gulped in oxygen with a cry of triumph. Below her the soldier, still dazed, carried on down to the bottom.

Sarah placed both of her hands on the metal frame of the next complete section and pushed herself up and out of the water. She landed on the slippery glass beside the soldier's fallen dart-rifle. Someone was approaching from behind, so Sarah closed her hands over the weapon and wheeled round. The other soldier stood there with his dart-rifle raised.

DON'T!

The soldier froze. Sarah aimed the dart-rifle at him, still gasping for breath.

Drop yours in the water. And the pistol.

Without a word, the soldier tossed his weapon into the broken section. It disappeared under the water. He then unclipped his pistol from its holster and tossed that as well.

Very good. Now sit down with your hands on your head.

Sarah laughed spontaneously as the soldier, muscle-bound and over two metres tall, sat down obediently before her. She lowered the dart-gun and shook her head.

"What are you doing?" Major Bright demanded excitedly, running up as the other soldier emerged from the tank, shaking his head in confusion. "Why did you throw away your weapons? Tell me!"

"I don't think they had much choice," a female voice said from the edge of the pool.

Both Sarah and Major Bright looked round at the person who'd spoken. She was an attractive woman dressed in a white lab coat. Sarah detected an air of authority about her that suggested she was more than just another HIDRA scientist, however. She was a little breathless, as if she'd been running, and there was anger in her eyes.

"I'm calling off this little experiment, Major Bright," the woman ordered, glaring at him.

"Colonel Moss wants results—" Bright began.

"That's enough, Major!" the woman interrupted, clearly trying hard to keep calm. "You seem to have forgotten I outrank you, even if I am a scientist."

Inside his helmet, Major Bright's face went a shade of red that bordered on purple, but he said nothing.

The woman ran a hand through her long, black hair and turned her attention to Sarah. She was about Major Bright's age, but her face was warmer, more intelligent. She certainly didn't look like any of the military people Sarah had met so far at HIDRA.

"Hi, my name's Rachel," the woman said with a smile. "I'm sorry we haven't met before now."

Sarah took a step forward and pointed the dart-gun at her. Rachel gestured to the open door behind her.

"Come on, I want to help you," she said. "How far do you really think you're going to get like that?"

Sarah looked at the weapon in her hand – not much use against all of HIDRA. The woman had a point. She lowered it.

Rachel smiled. "We've got a lot to talk about, Sarah. I'll leave your men to clean up this mess, Major."

He gave a grunt of disapproval.

Sarah looked from Rachel to Major Bright and back again. After a moment's consideration, she threw the dart-gun into his arms and walked to the edge of the tank. Rachel draped a towel over her shoulders and led her out of the building.

17

"Shouldn't I be in one of the bubbles?" Sarah asked as Rachel led her from the building across the HIDRA complex. It seemed strange to be walking around with nothing to separate her from the outside world. The atmosphere inside the dome was unexpectedly stuffy, as if it were full of air recycled too many times. There was something stale about it.

"Your tests came back negative," Rachel explained. "You're not a carrier any more and neither is Robert. So, no more bubbles."

Rachel led her to a small building and showed her inside. It was some kind of office, with computers, microscopes and other machines Sarah didn't recognize arranged on tables. There was also a television and DVD in one corner, next to a folding bed. Sarah frowned at the set-up as Rachel showed her over to a chair and flicked on a kettle.

"Do you live in here?" she asked as the woman fixed two mugs of instant coffee.

Rachel looked round the room and nodded with a faint smile.

"I don't get out much," she admitted.

"You're a scientist?" Sarah asked, looking along a line of expensive-looking microscopes. It was then she saw the name plaque next to the computer: *Dr. Rachel Andersen, Chief Scientist*.

"Oh, I see," Sarah said. "You're the one in charge here."

Rachel turned and handed her a mug. "I wouldn't say that. But I have some say in what goes on. Enough to put Major Bright in his place. He's Colonel Moss's second-in-command, but I outrank him."

"Was the water tank your idea or his?"

Rachel pulled up a chair and sat before her, cradling the coffee in her hands. She looked into Sarah's eyes.

"I didn't know that was going to happen. The moment I found out, I came running. Do you believe me?"

Sarah concentrated on Rachel and had the overwhelming impression she was telling the truth.

"I guess."

Rachel smiled. "Are you warm enough? How's the drink?"

"Very good," Sarah replied, taking another sip. Her eyes fell on a set of photographs pinned above a computer workstation: two girls about Robert's age in identical school uniforms. They were both dark-haired like Rachel and had her brown eyes.

Rachel followed Sarah's gaze. "My girls. Audrey and Katherine. They're nine and eleven."

"Are they here?" Sarah asked.

"No, with their father back in England," Rachel replied, sadness in her voice. "I get back to them as much as possible, but the fall virus has kept me pretty busy since the outbreak in South America. Looks like I won't be seeing them for a while now..."

"It must be hard for you," Sarah said. "To be so far away, I mean."

Rachel nodded and looked back at her. "It's the hardest thing in the world. But whenever I miss them too much, I think about what would happen if something like the fall virus found its way to Europe. That's what I'm working for – to keep them safe."

"So, you can't go home until you find the cure," Sarah said.

"Something like that."

"What do you want from me, Rachel?"

"I'd like you to tell me how you got out of the tank," the scientist replied bluntly.

Sarah shrugged. "The soldiers are the ones who broke the glass. Ask them."

"I don't think they'd be able to tell me themselves, do you? They didn't seem fully in control of their actions. I can help you, Sarah. But you have to start being honest with me. You must've worked out by now that the tests are about more than just finding a cure for the virus."

Sarah thought back to the sleep sensors, the room with the noise, the tank.

"Okay, let's do it like this," Rachel said finally. "I'll answer one of your questions truthfully for every one of mine you answer. Deal?"

Sarah thought for a moment. "Fine. What are—"

"And I get to ask the first question," Rachel interrupted, holding up a finger. "How did you get out of the tank?"

"I made the soldier shoot the glass," Sarah replied,

giving as little as possible. “What are you doing with Robert?”

“He’s safe, undergoing tests like you have. But I promise he won’t be put in the tank. Nobody will be again. How did you make the soldier do that?”

“I can do…things. I saw into his mind and made him draw his gun.”

Saying it out loud, it sounded unbelievable even to Sarah herself. However, Rachel merely sat back in her chair and nodded as if she’d been expecting such an answer.

“Why am I being kept apart from Robert?” she pressed.

Rachel regarded her evenly. “Because some people around here are afraid of what you might be able to do together. That’s why you’ve been isolated. Have you spoken to your brother since the tests began?”

“No,” Sarah began, but then corrected herself. “I hear his voice sometimes. In my head. Why are they afraid? Who’s afraid?”

Rachel grinned. “That’s two questions, so I’ll only answer one. Young people who come into contact with the fall virus and are immune to its effects tend to develop new abilities, just like the ones you’ve talked about. Mind-reading, telekinesis, telepathic communication – all possible side-effects for those who have immunity. Pretty scary, don't you think?"

"Yes," Sarah replied. "And I'm counting that as a question. So tell me who's afraid."

Rachel raised an eyebrow at that, but answered anyway. "Some of the soldiers. HIDRA is made up of both scientists, like me, and the military, like our friend Major Bright. Let's just say, each group has different ideas about how things should be run. What happened in the tank today isn't going to help. They probably won't like the idea of a fourteen-year-old girl being able to control where they point their guns."

"Then they shouldn't have tried to drown me, should they?" Sarah replied angrily. "Why did they do that?"

"The development of these abilities has been linked to traumatic events," Rachel explained, even though it was her turn to ask a question. "It seems that a highly stressful situation – like the water tank – can give the mind a push. Maybe it's the natural survival instinct forcing the body to use the power given by the virus. Colonel Moss developed the tank test after the Colombian meteorite. I hate to say it, but it seems to have worked with you, hasn't it?"

Sarah shook her head, remembering what happened when Colonel Moss told them about Daniel. That's when

Robert had first projected his thoughts into her mind. Was it the shock that broke his mental block? And she had to admit the tank had forced her to discover how to control the soldiers…

"That's horrible," she said. "And you work for that guy?"

"Colonel Moss's methods have become very questionable since the Colombian meteorite," Rachel said, leaning forward in her chair. "But he still has the support of some influential people. That's why I believe I can do more good on the inside of HIDRA. When I have enough evidence against him, I'll make sure he's removed."

Sarah looked at her sceptically. She was getting used to not trusting anyone around the base.

Rachel seemed to read her thoughts. "Look into my mind, Sarah. You'll see I'm on your side…"

Sarah hesitated for a moment, before focusing her attention on Rachel, picking a spot between her eyes. Slowly, images began to form, as if a wireless connection was downloading them directly into her brain. At first they were a confused jumble, just as when she had connected with the soldier, but this time Sarah found she could sort them more quickly. One image stood out from the rest and she zeroed in on it, until it filled her consciousness. She closed her eyes…

Inside a building Sarah has never seen… Rachel stands opposite Colonel Moss, hands on her hips…

"I want to know why we're putting these children through this, Colonel," she demands. Behind her, Sarah can make out monitors showing children in other rooms. Some are sleeping, while others are being attended by suited scientists – all are alone…

"The side-effects have priority, Dr. Andersen," Colonel Moss replies curtly, as if this is a conversation they've had before.

"HIDRA's primary objective is finding a cure for the virus," Rachel protests. "General Wellman made it perfectly clear—"

"General Wellman is sixteen thousand kilometres away," Colonel Moss interrupts. "As long as we contain the virus to mainland Australia, the general will be perfectly happy. You might have his ear at the Paris HQ, but you're a long way from there now and way out of your depth."

The colonel opens a drawer and pulls out a wad of email printouts. He throws them on the desk. Rachel runs her hand over them.

"You've been intercepting my emails?" she says, anger rising in her voice. "This is a gross breach of privacy, Colonel. On what grounds have you done this?"

"I don't mind you going behind my back to the general," Moss continues, ignoring her question. "Now, what did you write again...?"

"That your methods are questionable," Rachel replies. "And that you seem to have lost sight of our humanitarian objective."

Colonel Moss's blue eyes are as hard as diamonds. "What disappoints me, Rachel, is that you can't see that we're in the middle of something bigger than finding vaccinations for a few civilians. We're at the start of a war, and you're either with us or against us."

Rachel shakes her head. "Our only priority is the sleepers! We've got an epidemic on our hands."

Colonel Moss slams his fist on the desk. "HIDRA's priority is whatever I say it is. This is a military–scientific operation, Dr. Andersen, but the military comes first. The power those children are developing is a weapon, whether you want to acknowledge that or not. Either we unlock the secrets of that weapon, or the wrong people will. We've been getting nowhere with the Williams girl. I've decided it's time to push a little harder."

"What are you talking about?" Rachel demands.

"Traumatic events clearly force their abilities to new heights," Colonel Moss states. "Telekinesis. Telepathy. The CIA has been trying to develop this for sixty years!

Putting those kids under stress can yield excellent results, as we saw with the Colombian boys..."

"The tank!" gasps Rachel. "I won't allow it again..."

"Too late," Colonel Moss replies. "The girl is already being processed."

Rachel runs from the room...

Sarah opened her eyes again and the images faded.

"The colonel – why did you want me to see that?" she asked.

"Because I want you to trust me," Rachel replied. "Not everyone here is like Colonel Moss and Major Bright. As soon as I can get enough evidence to use against him, I'm going to make sure he loses his command. But for the moment he's in control. That means we have to work with him."

Sarah looked round the office – so cramped and small compared to Colonel Moss.

"Why don't your people just take over?" she asked.

Rachel shook her head. "Again, my people are scientists – not fighters. The majority of HIDRA soldiers are just following orders, but the colonel's Special Forces are one hundred per cent behind him. Colonel Moss isn't just going to relinquish command because a few scientists ask him to – and don't think for a moment they wouldn't use force to put down a mutiny.

Right now, we can achieve more by playing along with the colonel."

Sarah nodded, trying to make sense of everything she was being told. Colonel Moss was clearly taking advantage of the crisis and their isolation in the desert to do whatever he pleased. Suddenly she was a bit more scared of him than she had been before. Hearing the woman describe their situation made it very real.

Rachel stood and walked to the door. "Come on. There's something else I have to show you."

18

Rachel led her to a small room in another building. There were cameras, monitors and a long window which looked into a white room. A girl who looked about eight sat on the edge of a bed, leafing listlessly through the pages of a book. She brushed away the long blonde hair from her face and looked directly at them, revealing the most unusual eyes – one iris was green and one was blue. The effect was startling and for a moment Sarah thought the girl saw them, but quickly realized they were on the other side of a two-way mirror like the one in her room. The girl looked back at the book.

Rachel tapped on the shoulder of a woman sitting in front of one of the monitors.

"Give us ten minutes," she ordered.

The woman rose and looked round at them both with a frown. Sarah noticed the woman's security pass lying on the desk. *Magda Stepnik.* She moved to stand in front of it.

"Colonel Moss said this one was not to leave my sight," the woman said, her accent eastern-European.

Rachel glanced at Sarah and then back at Magda. "That's an order."

The other woman looked for a moment as if she was going to argue, but finally rose from the chair and stomped out of the room. "I'll wait in the corridor."

"You do that," Rachel said coldly. Behind her back, Sarah palmed the forgotten security card.

"What was that about?" she asked Rachel.

The doctor sighed and took the vacated chair. "The colonel has his spies among the scientists, too. I know who they are, but for the moment..." She shrugged.

Sarah nodded and turned her attention to the girl on the other side of the glass.

"Louise," Rachel said into the microphone. The girl looked up.

"Hello?" she said. "Where's Magda?"

"Magda's busy at the moment," Rachel replied. "How are you feeling today, Louise?"

The girl jumped off the bed and walked to the mirror.

"I want to see Dad. I don't want to stay in here alone." Her voice broke a little.

"Your dad's not well at the moment, Louise, you know that." Rachel's voice was firm, but showed concern. "But would you like it if I could find a friend for you? Someone to play with? How does that sound?"

Louise looked at the mirror, her face brightening.

"Can she stay?"

"She can stay with you as long as she likes," Rachel replied, glancing at Sarah. "I'll ask her if she'd like to visit."

Rachel placed her hand over the mic and said softly, "She's lost her father to the virus and she needs someone to be her friend. Someone she can trust."

Sarah shook her head. "I'm not her mother," she said.

"Our people are scientists and soldiers, you've seen that," Rachel replied. "They don't understand children. Look at Louise, Sarah. She's all alone. She's hearing voices in her head and needs someone who understands what's happening to her."

"And I guess you'd want me to report anything else I notice while I'm with her," Sarah added.

Rachel sighed. "You're right, that's what you'd have to do, Sarah. But you'd be saving her from the attentions of Major Bright. If you can find out information about Louise and her developing powers, it'll keep Colonel Moss's men off our backs for a while. Maybe long enough for my scientists to develop a cure. When we have that, perhaps I'll be able to persuade the general to throw Colonel Moss out."

"And what if I say no?" Sarah held Rachel's eyes defiantly.

Rachel regarded her evenly. "Do you want to see your brother or not? I can get you one hour with him for every hour you work with Louise. Colonel Moss will allow that. Even he knows we need help. It's the best I can do right now."

Sarah looked away. The idea of helping Colonel Moss in any way didn't make her feel good, but she needed to see Robert. And maybe if she made contact with other children on the base there might be the chance to...

"Make your mind up, Sarah," Rachel demanded. "You have to meet me halfway here."

Sarah nodded finally. "I'll need some other things as well."

"Okay."

"I want out of this hospital smock."

"Right. I'll get you some clothes."

"And I want some music."

"I'll get you an iPod. Anything else?"

"That's all – for now," Sarah replied.

With that, Rachel pressed a button by the window and a door appeared in the wall, revealing a corridor. The doctor placed a restraining hand on Sarah's shoulder as she was about to leave the room. She froze, gripping Magda's security pass tighter in her hands.

"Thank you," Rachel said. "You're doing a good thing here."

Sarah nodded and moved forward. A door at the end of the corridor slid open and she stepped into Louise's room. The younger girl looked at her with surprise and shock.

"I don't know you," she whispered.

"It's okay," Sarah said, walking further inside. The door closed and locked with a click. Louise let out a scream and backed into the nearest corner. Sarah stopped in her tracks, deciding to try a different approach.

It's okay, Louise. I'm a friend. My name's Sarah.

The girl looked at Sarah, eyes widening.

You can talk too!

Sarah smiled.

Yes. So can my brother.

I thought it was just me and Wei.

Who's Wei?

Louise pointed to the wall. *He's over there somewhere. We talk sometimes. I thought you were one of them. They hurt me.*

Louise rubbed her arm as she said the last sentence. Sarah nodded and held out her own arm, showing the bruises caused where they'd taken repeated blood samples.

They've hurt me too.

Louise walked towards Sarah and reached out to touch her hand.

I'm sorry I screamed before, Louise said. *I'm not supposed to, I know.*

Why's that? asked Sarah.

Bad things happen when I get upset. Things get broken. I broke the mirror once...

Sarah looked round at the mirror in the wall, sensing Rachel watching them behind it.

How did you do that?

I just got really angry and it started to crack all over... I'm not even supposed to talk about it...

Sarah sensed Louise starting to get upset, so she

decided to change the subject. She saw pens and sheets of paper laid out on the bed. She picked one up and looked at the picture Louise had drawn: it showed a girl standing next to the towering figure of a man.

Is that your dad? Sarah asked.

Louise looked down and shook her head. *No, Colonel Moss. I don't like him.*

Sarah picked up a blank piece of paper and a pencil.

Then why don't we draw a picture together? A nicer one.

Louise smiled and nodded.

As they sat down together, Sarah cast a look at the mirror, aware of Rachel on the other side. Out of sight, she slid Magda's security pass from her hand and under the mattress for safe keeping.

19

"I don't like this game," Louise said with a pout. "It's boring."

"I know, but just one more time," Sarah said, shaking the pieces from the jigsaw frame onto the floor. "Then we can go on SingStar again."

Louise sighed theatrically, but nodded. Sarah laid the frame between them and sat back. Louise crossed her legs on the floor and closed her eyes. One by one, the jigsaw pieces began to lift into the air and float across to the frame. It was a toddler's puzzle – only ten pieces. Nevertheless, the second and third pieces went in face down.

"*Louise*," Sarah warned. "Do it properly."

"Okay, okay," the other girl replied with a sigh. The pieces rearranged themselves quickly. The rest of the puzzle was solved within a few seconds. Louise opened her eyes and looked at Sarah. "Happy now?"

Sarah put the completed jigsaw to one side. "Excellent work. How do you do that?"

Louise shrugged. "I just close my eyes and picture the pieces on the ground. Then I imagine them going where I want. And it happens."

Sarah glanced at the mirror. Testing was over for that day – the third session she'd spent with Louise. It gave her a bad feeling to be conducting tests like the jigsaw – making it seem like a game for Louise – but it was all part of the deal she'd made with Rachel. She knew that in the room next door, they'd be taping everything during her and Louise's "play session".

"I'm going first!" Louise said, jumping up and grabbing the microphone near the games console. They'd got her some more toys at Sarah's request and SingStar was a favourite. Louise used the controller to select the same song she'd been performing all morning: "Never Gonna Give You Up".

"Not that one again," Sarah groaned. "Don't you want to choose something newer? Have a bit of a change?"

Louise lowered the mic in her hand and looked at Sarah, tears forming in her eyes. "It was my dad's favourite. He used to play it in the car all the time."

"Oh, I see," Sarah began, placing a comforting hand on Louise's shoulder…

A stream of images flooded her mind…

The interior of a car… Dust swirls around the windows, almost obscuring the desert beyond… A dark-haired man slumps over the wheel…

Figures approach through the sandstorm – suited and recognizable as mirror-masks… Then they're in the car, dragging the man away…

Louise's voice cries out, "Stop that! Leave my dad alone!"

Now she's outside the car... A mirror-mask tries to grab her… She raises a hand…

"No!"

The mirror-mask flies back into the sandstorm, as if pushed by a massive, unseen force… The other suits look at one another and then move in…

"I said no!"

One of them makes a lunge at her, but Louise screams… The mirrored faceplate of his helmet explodes outwards…

Sarah tore her hand away and blinked at Louise in surprise.

"Are you okay, Sarah?" Louise asked quietly.

"Yeah," Sarah said with a nod. "I might just sit down for a moment."

She moved to the bed, still a little shaky from the experience. It had felt as if Louise's memories were drowning her. The girl's thoughts had an intensity that hadn't been there when she'd connected with Rachel. It was almost scary.

"I felt you inside my mind," the other girl said. "How do you do that?"

Sarah shook her head. "I don't even know yet. I saw you – what were you doing out in the desert?"

"We were driving to Perth," Louise replied. "Dad wanted to drive all round the country. He said I should see every state before I was ten. He..."

Her voice cracked and Sarah held out her arms to hug her, being careful not to touch the girl with her bare hands. Sarah had learned one thing that day: intense emotions could be suffocating with her sensitive new power.

"They took him away," Louise sobbed into her shoulder. "Colonel Moss said I couldn't be with him because I hurt the people who tried to rescue us. But I didn't mean to."

"It's okay," Sarah soothed. "You were just afraid. We're going to learn how to control our powers, just you see. Then everything will be okay."

"Promise?" Louise mumbled.

"Promise."

Half an hour later, Sarah left Louise's room and was met in the corridor by a white-coated HIDRA scientist who asked her question after question about the session. Sarah had sensed the anger in the other girl and her fear for her dad, who had been sent somewhere by Colonel Moss. Now Sarah also sensed the fear in the scientists around her.

They're afraid of us, she thought.

"Tell me about her powers," the scientist demanded. "Have you observed a strengthening in her telekinetic ability? Has she moved anything larger than the jigsaw pieces with her mind?"

Sarah shrugged. "You're the ones watching through the mirror. You should've seen."

"Does she seem angry?"

"She wants to see her dad."

"That's not possible. He's been relocated. Now, tell me about..."

So it went on. After the questions, Sarah was finally allowed to see Robert again. Two soldiers escorted her across the dome to the building where her brother was being kept.

Sarah!

Robert flew across the room and threw his arms around her. She stroked a hand through his hair.

It's okay. I'm here now.

They had an hour together. At Sarah's direction, they spoke out loud about "safe" subjects: the food, things that Robert wanted for his room, games they could play. In their minds, however, they exchanged all the information they didn't want Robert's "mirror watcher", Michael, to hear. He talked about the tests to which they'd subjected him, holding back tears as he did so.

We're getting out of here, Sarah told him while they played cards together on the edge of his bed. *I just need a little time to find a way. I think Louise might be able to help. They're afraid of her power.*

Robert shifted uneasily. *They keep on asking me what I can do. They try to get me to move things, or read their minds, but I can't. They said the virus has changed us, but all I can do is speak to you.*

It's okay, Sarah reassured. *There's nothing wrong with you. But we can't stay here. They're not good people.*

She thought of Colonel Moss, and then Rachel. *Well, most of them aren't, anyway.*

What about Daniel?

Sarah placed a hand on his arm. *He's got the virus, Robert. He isn't coming back. We're going to have to look after ourselves now.*

At that, Robert began to cry quietly and she put her arms around him once more. Too soon, the voice of Michael from the mirror told her it was time to go and the door opened.

Don't go! Her brother tried to hold her back as she rose.

I have to, Robert, Sarah said firmly. *They won't let me come back if we cause trouble. I'm going to find a way for us to escape, but you have to be strong until then. Can you do that for me?*

He wiped his eyes and nodded seriously. Sarah squeezed his hand and left the room.

20

Sarah lay awake in the darkness. Under the bed-sheets she turned the stolen security pass over and over in her hands, but her mind was focused on the woman sitting on the other side of the mirror. Sarah called her Mandy2, because she worked the night shift watching her. Mandy2 had never bothered to introduce herself properly and Sarah hadn't asked for her name either.

In her mind, Sarah sensed Mandy2 staring at the darkened room... The boredom and fatigue... Her eyes beginning to close, just like they always did at some point in the night...

Sarah waited until she was fully asleep before easing herself out of the bed. Taking one of the pillows, she placed it under the cover. If Mandy2 did wake up, she might be fooled into thinking she was still there for a while by the bulge. It was hard to see in the darkness.

Pleased with her handiwork, Sarah moved swiftly to the door with Magda's key card in her hand. However, she paused before she swept it through the reader – for all she knew it was only good for Louise's door. Perhaps it would even trigger an alert. Deciding it was worth the risk, she swiped the card...

The door opened silently and she slipped through. Sarah held her breath for a second in the corridor, fully expecting the place to light up with alarms. It didn't happen. She breathed again, casting her mind back to the room. Mandy2 was still sleeping and hopefully would be for the next hour, just like most nights. Enough time for Sarah to find out a bit more about the base and then sneak back into the room unseen. She moved towards the exit.

The dome was in semi-darkness. It was the first time Sarah had been out of her room at such a late hour and she was pleased to see they created a "night" in the dome as well. It gave her cover as she ran from building to building. She stopped beside one of those with sarcophagi inside and peered round the edge. In the distance she saw the main airlock – the only way in or out of the dome. Her heart sank when she saw the number of guards patrolling the area: six at least, even at night, all Special Forces.

She cast her mind around the dome, looking for anything of interest. It didn't take long for her thoughts to centre on a building over to her right. She sensed the presence of Colonel Moss inside and realized that it was the place where he'd argued with Rachel. Two guards passed close by her hiding place but didn't see her in the shadows. Sarah waited for them to go before sprinting across the open area to the building. She pressed herself against the wall in the shadows and focused on the people inside…

Colonel Moss sits at a desk facing Rachel… She paces angrily before him…

"…just where are you getting your orders from, Colonel?" she says, voice full of anger. "HIDRA is meant to be helping the victims of the virus, but you're turning this operation into a weapons research project…"

"I'm doing what's necessary to maintain control of this situation," he interrupts. "Sit down Dr. Andersen.

I'm getting sick of these scenes."

"I won't," Rachel replies. "I don't like how you're handling the children and neither do my team."

"I gave you Sarah Williams, didn't I? I stopped the tank experiments. What more do you want?"

"I want your guarantee that no more of them will be harmed. Using Sarah to report on Louise's abilities is yielding results. I want her to spend time with more of the children..."

Colonel Moss sighs and leafs through a report on his desk.

"I've seen the answers she gave your team," he says with contempt. "Nothing we didn't know already. I'm going to give you another day to get something I can use, then we return to my methods..."

Sarah momentarily lost control of the vision as she thought back to the tank. One day! She had to find a way out of the dome sooner rather than later. She focused on the room again.

"My people won't stand for that, Colonel," Rachel replies. "These children have parents and they should be allowed to be with them, even if they're victims of the virus."

Colonel Moss sits back in his chair. "Just get me results. Information about how their powers work. One more day, Dr. Andersen."

Rachel shakes her head and walks from the room without another word.

Outside the building, Sarah held her breath as the doctor emerged. Rachel was too preoccupied with her own thoughts to notice her, however. As the woman strode off across the dome, Sarah turned her attention back to the colonel.

Moss rubs his eyes as a third person emerges from the shadows and stands to attention. Major Bright.

"I take it you heard all that," Colonel Moss says. "I'm beginning to regret not removing her when we found out about the emails to Wellman. Too bad we need her to keep the scientists in line."

"She's trouble, sir," Major Bright responds. "But she's right. The scientists are starting to make noises. Our insiders on the science team have the names of the main trouble-makers. They can be easily neutralized."

"And the men?"

"Special Forces can keep the normal soldiers in line, Colonel," Major Bright states firmly.

Colonel Moss rises from his chair. "The way the Williams girl got out of that tank was...impressive. Hell, she might become as powerful as Octavio. I want that power, and no bleeding-heart bunch of scientists is going to get in the way."

"Just tell me what you want to do, sir."

Colonel Moss runs a hand over his scalp. "The sleeper subjects are an unnecessary complication. Start shipping them out to the civilian hospitals. That should keep the scientists busy while we prep for the next stage of the Superhuman project. By the time General Wellman finds out what's going on, we'll have our results. There have been no reports of Daniel Williams' body being found yet?"

Major Bright shuffles on the spot uneasily. "No, sir. As you know, two of our men took him out to the desert two days ago... They haven't returned."

Moss looks at his second-in-command with ice in his eyes. "And you wait until now to tell me this, Major?"

Bright stiffens to attention. "I sent two of our best, sir. Williams would be no match for them. Our men must have been delayed. I've already sent a second patrol to find them."

"Make sure they do," Moss barks. "I want Williams confirmed dead and his children... What's that?"

Sarah snapped out of the vision with a jolt. The sound of an alarm carried across the dome. She heard a door being opened in the building and ran.

All around her, the dome burst into life as the lights, previously dimmed to create twilight, were thrown on full. Instantly it was daytime again and Sarah found that her shadowy hiding places were gone. Reaching the side of another building, she looked around desperately. *They'd killed Daniel!* Her heart was racing, but she tried to control herself. First, she had to get to Robert. She looked around the dome, searching for him with her mind.

His building was maybe a hundred metres away. She ran for it, aware of soldiers approaching from all directions.

Reaching Robert's building, she burst through the main door and found herself in a deserted corridor with three unmarked doors. Robert was behind the third one, Sarah sensed. Heart racing, she tried swiping the stolen ID card to open it, but nothing happened. She tried again and again, with no result. The card must have been locked out. Sarah slammed her fist onto the door and slumped against the wall.

Sarah! Sarah! I hear you!

She looked at the door, pressing her palms to the cool, plastic material.

Robert!

Get me out of here!

Sarah could sense the panic building in him. The continual tests had been hard for her to endure, but he was so many years younger.

The sound of a door opening caused Sarah to spin

round in time to see a scientist approaching from one of the other rooms, a sleep aerosol raised to spray. In a flash, Sarah's pent-up anger directed fully towards the man and he froze in his tracks, eyes wide with fear as her feelings surged through his mind. She visualized the hand holding the aerosol moving round...

Struggling against himself, the scientist pointed the aerosol spray in his face and pushed the trigger. He crashed to the ground.

Sarah, you've got to run! They're coming!

Sarah sensed it too. At least three soldiers were approaching the building.

I'm not leaving you, she told Robert.

Just run!

They lied to us about taking care of Daniel. Don't trust any of them. I'll be back for you…

With that, she bolted for the exit, dashing out past one of the soldiers, almost knocking him over as she went. Hands grabbed at her, but she ran on blindly, evading them and making for the edge of the dome. Maybe she'd be able to cut her way through somehow… A new voice broke through her thoughts.

Over here. Keep running...

It was a male voice. She slowed for a moment, looking for the direction from which it had come.

By the truck. Move!

The voice again, directing her towards a huge, camouflaged truck parked by the dome wall. She doubled her pace, aware of soldiers gaining on her.

An arm shot out as she passed the side of the vehicle, dragging her round and down by the wheels. A hand clamped over her mouth. She turned to find herself looking into a pair of brown eyes belonging to a boy her own age, his skin and hair darker than hers.

He held up a finger to his lips as two soldiers began to pace around the truck. At any moment, Sarah expected them to check under the wheels, but they didn't. One of them spoke into a communications device, receiving orders. A second later both soldiers walked away. The blaring alarms around the dome stopped abruptly.

Come on, the boy ordered without speaking aloud, pulling her out from under the truck. They made for a smaller building near the wall and ran through the open door.

Inside, Sarah blinked as her eyes adjusted to the dimness. Her rescuer stepped into the room and closed the door. She looked around, making out two beds and a television. Computer games and books were strewn about on the floor.

Another boy appeared from the shadows. He looked almost identical to the other, except his features were a little sharper and his eyes a little harder.

"I'm Octavio," he said. "And this is my brother, Nestor. What took you so long to get here?"

21

"Who are you?" Sarah demanded, stepping back against the door. "Why did you bring me here?"

She took another look around their room. It was nothing like the cold hospital cell she'd been given. The walls were lined with posters and shelves of books. A case of DVDs stood near the beds.

"It's okay," reassured Nestor, the one who'd grabbed her. His voice had a definite accent to it. Spanish-sounding. "We just want to help you."

His brother, Octavio, produced a deck of cards from

his pocket and held up one of them in his slender hand, its back to her. Sarah felt for the handle of the door and turned it. It was locked.

"Let me out of here," she said, looking from one boy to the other.

"You can go," Octavio said slowly, pushing past his brother with the card held out. "All you have to do is tell me what card I'm holding."

Sarah shook her head and side-stepped him, moving back into the room, almost tripping on the clutter on the floor.

"I don't know what you're talking about," she said. "I'm not doing anything you say."

Nestor looked at his brother, "Take it easy, Octavio. Can't you see she's scared?"

"All she has to do is show us what she can do," Octavio said relentlessly. "Then she can go."

Sarah reached out and snatched the card from his hand, looking at it.

"Three of clubs!" she cried, throwing it back in his face. "Now let me out of here. I have to get my brother!"

Octavio calmly held up another card. His eyes were cruel and intense.

"Tell me and you can go."

Sarah looked into his eyes angrily, concentrating on

the card. The image on the other side started to appear, a blur at first, then becoming clearer.

"The king of diamonds," she said, looking at Nestor, who hovered uncomfortably at his brother's shoulder.

"Well done," replied Octavio with a nod. He produced another one from the deck. "She's fast, Nestor. Potentially powerful psionic ability. What about this card?"

Nestor walked to the door and pressed a button on the wall to unlock it.

"She did what you wanted, Octavio," he said, holding the door open. "You can go, Sarah."

She took a step towards the door, then stopped and turned on them both.

"How do you know my name?" she demanded. "How come you two are living like this when the rest of the survivors are locked up in cells?"

Octavio gave a little laugh. He sat on the edge of the bed and lounged back, shuffling the cards expertly in his hands.

"We're not survivors," he explained. "At least, not of this meteorite. We've been with Colonel Moss for a while. Waiting to meet more people like us."

People who have the power. It was Nestor's voice in her head.

What's happening to me? Sarah asked him. She decided that she liked Nestor a whole lot more than his brother.

The virus, he explained. *It seems to create a kind of link between anyone exposed to it. And much more besides.*

At least for those not put into a coma by it, Octavio interrupted. *The virus gives us powers. It's different for everyone. Let me show you...*

Octavio tossed the cards in the air. He held out his hand and they hung suspended. The cards circled around, picking up speed as they went, controlled by the boy's telekinetic power. His ability reminded Sarah of Louise, although he clearly had greater control over it. The cards started to shoot out in various directions like tiny missiles. One of them grazed her cheek.

That's enough, Octavio! Stop showing off!

Nestor's hand shot out and the cards were thrown against the back wall by a powerful blast of air. The brothers faced each other for a second, eyes locked together in anger. The temperature in the room had dropped by ten degrees in as many seconds and Sarah sensed that it was Nestor's doing. There was a low rumble in the room – like a sound of thunder before a coming storm.

"What's the deal with you two?" Sarah asked out loud,

stepping between them. "Did Colonel Moss give you all this stuff? Where are your parents?"

Nestor looked round at her. His face softened and immediately the atmosphere in the room returned to normal. The storm had passed, much to Sarah's relief.

"They didn't survive the Colombian meteorite," he explained. "Colonel Moss must have told you about the virus outbreak in South America, right?"

Sarah nodded and he continued, "The colonel looks after us now. We travel around, looking for other survivors."

"I thought HIDRA was supposed to be looking for a cure," Sarah asked.

"Maybe at first," Nestor explained. "But then Colonel Moss found out about our powers. The way we communicate with each other. How we can move things..."

Now he wants what we have, Octavio finished. He swept his arm around the room. *This is what we get in return for...cooperation. If we didn't, Moss would have us in cages. Just like you and your brother.*

Sarah shook her head. "We have to get out of here. All of us. You two, Robert. And there are more kids like us in this base. You must know better than me."

Nestor nodded. He explained that there were six of

them in total. At fourteen, Sarah and the Colombian twins were the oldest, while Louise was the youngest. All of them, apart from Nestor and Octavio, were survivors of the meteorite crash in the Australian desert. And all of them were starting to develop powers. Colonel Moss had been careful to keep them apart, separated from one another while his men observed how powerful they were actually becoming.

Sarah listened intently to what he had to say.

When he finished she said, "Look, we can make it out of here if we work together. That's what Colonel Moss and the soldiers are afraid of. Some of the scientists want to help us too!"

Octavio stood and looked towards the door.

I'm afraid it's too late for that, he said solemnly.

Heavy footsteps approached from outside and Sarah's warning signal went off in her mind. She looked round and backed away as the figure of Colonel Moss appeared in the doorway.

"Stay away from me," she ordered, concentrating on him. *Take out your gun and toss it on the floor, Colonel.*

Colonel Moss smiled coldly and stepped into the room.

"That trick isn't going to work with me," he replied. "I've had enough practice with Octavio to be able to shield my mind from your type. I was impressed to hear how you escaped from the water tank, among other things. Now you're going to show me what else you can do."

Sarah looked at Nestor, who couldn't meet her gaze. She turned her attention back to Colonel Moss.

"And what if I refuse?"

Colonel Moss pulled out a chair from the computer desk and sat down.

"That would be a disappointing decision," he replied, not taking his eyes from her. "Boys, why don't you give us some privacy?"

Nestor looked as if he was going to protest, but Octavio caught his arm and pulled him from the room. As they left, another figure appeared – Major Bright. He stepped inside, then closed and locked the door.

"You have to realize that I only want what's best for everyone, Sarah," Colonel Moss said, trying to sound reasonable. "Octavio understands that cooperating with me makes sense. I think that he and Nestor are very happy here. Goodness knows what would have happened to them on the outside world. Branded as freaks, maybe. Or made to perform by ruthless people only interested in making money from their talents. You can trust me, Sarah..."

He reached out to touch her hand, but Sarah flinched away.

"I know what you did to Daniel," she said, unable to disguise the hatred in her voice. "I heard your conversation."

Colonel Moss winced. Anger flashed in his eyes and Sarah moved away from him on the edge of the bed.

"Eavesdroppers hear no good," Major Bright said softly from the door, as he traced a finger down the scar on his cheek.

"That really is too bad," Colonel Moss said with a nod. "I would have preferred to do this nicely. But I guess it's too late for that now. *Major.*"

Bright advanced swiftly, extracting something from his pocket as he did so. He placed a restraining hand on Sarah's shoulder and jabbed something into her exposed arm before she could react. She saw him depress the plunger of a syringe.

"What was that?" she asked, rubbing her arm as Major Bright stepped away. A wave of fear spread through her. *Had they just killed her?*

"Please, don't be alarmed," Colonel Moss said, raising his hand. "We've just given you something that will make you a little more cooperative."

Sarah's vision swam momentarily and she had to

struggle to keep her focus on Moss. A strange warmth spread up her arm from where the needle had entered. She knew she was in trouble, but was having difficulty remembering what it was. Her hand slipped off the edge of the bed and she giggled as she tried to right herself.

"I'm not going to help either of you," she replied with great effort, her voice sounding thick and slurred. "You're murderers..."

Colonel Moss smiled at her and leaned forward in his chair. His face suddenly seemed to fill the whole room. When he spoke his voice echoed through her head. There was no escape from it.

"You *will* help us, Sarah," he ordered. "Firstly, you're going to tell us what you discussed with Dr. Andersen. Then, you're going to show us all your special powers."

Sarah frowned at the colonel. Doing exactly what he wanted suddenly seemed like the best idea in the world. In fact, she couldn't remember why she'd ever tried to keep secrets from him in the first place.

"Okay," she whispered. Her voice sounded as if it were coming from the end of a very long tunnel.

Colonel Moss sat back in his chair and made his fingers into a steeple before him.

"Now, tell me about Rachel Andersen..."

22

"We're going to have to keep you on a tighter leash from now on I'm afraid, Sarah," Colonel Moss said with sadness in his voice. "We can't have children running around in the dome wherever they want. They might get hurt."

He stood next to the mirror in her room while a woman Sarah hadn't seen before pulled the bedclothes around her. She tried to remember how she'd got back from Nestor and Octavio's room, but found her memory a blur.

"What happened?" she asked weakly. When she tried to move her arms she found them restrained. She looked down at the bed and saw thick, plastic straps holding her in place.

"Don't be alarmed," Colonel Moss said, walking closer to the bed. "They're just until I know I can trust you again. With good behaviour, you'll have all your old privileges back in no time. Just keep on helping out with Louise and you'll find me very generous. She and the others are going to need you more than ever now. I'm afraid we're going to step up the Superhuman project. Dr. Andersen isn't going to be holding us back any more."

"Rachel?" Sarah managed. Her eyelids felt so heavy. She barely registered as someone else flew into the room through the open door.

"Well, speak of the devil," Colonel Moss said with a humourless laugh.

Rachel kneeled next to the bed and placed a hand on Sarah's forehead.

"What have you done to her? Has she been drugged? Colonel, this is the limit. My people simply won't stand for..."

Moss sighed and walked to the door. "I'll be waiting for you outside, Dr. Andersen. You have one minute before I send my men in here after you. Try not to upset the patient, eh?"

With that, he disappeared. Rachel looked back at Sarah and ran her hands over the restraints. She began to pull at one of the buckles to release it…

"I can't let you do that," the nurse said from the door. "Colonel's orders."

Rachel stared at the woman with anger in her eyes, but left the strap in place. She leaned closer to Sarah so she could whisper.

"I'm going to get you out of this," she said. "Colonel Moss has gone too far. I won't let him hurt you again."

Sarah felt a wetness running down her cheeks. She realized that she must be crying.

"Daniel…" she managed to say before she passed out once more.

Rachel exploded from the building in pursuit of Colonel Moss. Halfway to his office, she was intercepted by two soldiers – Special Forces. They grabbed her arms, but she pulled away violently.

"Take your hands off me, I'm the chief scientist," she retorted, rounding on the nearest one. The soldier looked at her impassively.

"Just come with us, Dr. Andersen," the other ordered. "The colonel's orders."

Rachel shook her head and continued in the direction she'd been going anyway. On the threshold of Moss's office she stopped to stare at one of the other buildings. Soldiers were carrying out caskets containing the sleepers and loading them into trucks.

"What the hell is going on?" she demanded.

"Major Bright's orders," the soldier answered. "The patients are being shipped out. Local services are going to take care of them now."

"And what about finding our cure?" Rachel demanded, but realized from the professionally blank look on the soldier's face that she was talking to the wrong person.

Inside the office, Colonel Moss was waiting for her. His second-in-command hung around in the corner like a bad smell.

"What are you playing at?" she demanded. "I'm calling Paris. General Wellman will want to know what's going on here."

She reached for the phone on his desk, but Moss slammed his hand down on the receiver before she could pick it up.

"The general is more concerned about keeping the virus out of Europe than talking to you," he snapped.

"In fact, he's placed HIDRA under full military control. That means your people report directly to me henceforth. The base is in lockdown: no one calls in or out, all network use is suspended until the crisis is over. General's orders."

"I don't believe you."

Colonel Moss rose from his chair. "I persuaded General Wellman that HIDRA's main interest should be the remarkable powers of these children rather than finding a cure for the disease. The local emergency services and army can take care of the coma victims. From now on we focus on harnessing the children's power. He's very excited about the generation of superhuman soldiers we're going to create. Even if we have to take those children apart piece by piece, we're going to find out their secret. And replicate it."

Rachel shook her head. "*Take them apart?* We're facing a global epidemic! General Wellman knows that the cure is our best weapon against the virus..."

Colonel Moss leaned across the desk and looked her hard in the eyes. "Are you calling me a liar, Dr. Andersen? I've had men shot for less."

Rachel stepped away from the table. "You're crazy, Colonel. I mean, you've lost it."

She backed into Major Bright, who had moved to

block her retreat. A classic pincer movement. Moss flashed an ice-cold smile.

Rachel shook her head. "My people will—"

"Do exactly as they're told," Moss snapped, expression ice-cold. "In fact, they're already working on a sample of Sarah Williams' blood. You're going to isolate the part of the virus that gives her those powers and inject it into one of my men."

Rachel laughed in disbelief. "What kind of fool would agree to be infected with the virus? Not even your Special Forces would follow you so blindly."

Moss gestured towards Bright. "But we already have our first volunteer. So go and make sure everything is ready for the procedure. It would be best for both you and your scientists, believe me."

Rachel turned and shook her head. "You're both mad."

Bright smiled and caught her arm.

"You're going to turn me into Superman, Dr. Andersen," he said softly. "And it had better work."

23

“Are you going to give us any more trouble today, Sarah?” Mandy’s voice cooed from the mirror.

Sarah stared at the ceiling and clenched her fists. She had to bite her lip to stop from screaming.

“Well?” Mandy persisted. “Louise is expecting you.”

Sarah let out a long, slow breath. “No.”

The soldier in the doorway advanced and unbuckled the restraints holding her to the bed. Sarah rubbed some circulation back into her arms.

“How long do I have to be strapped down like that?” she asked.

"Until Colonel Moss knows he can trust you," Mandy answered. "You see, Sarah, things are much nicer when you cooperate."

Sarah stared into the mirror. "I need to pee."

The soldier led her across the dome towards Louise's building, keeping a tight grip on her arm at all times, as if he expected her to make a run for it at any moment. Halfway across the dome, a Special Forces soldier blocked their way.

"Where are you taking this one?" he demanded.

"To see the telekinoid in 23B," the soldier holding Sarah replied and was waved on.

Sarah looked round at the man holding her. *The telekinoid? Is that their name for us?*

"This is Colonel Moss," an announcement boomed across the dome. "I would remind you that due to the attempted terrorist infiltration, this base has been placed under Special Forces command until further notice. Science personnel are required to carry permission documents for movement around the base. General military personnel are to follow the directives of Special Forces operatives, regardless of rank."

Terrorist infiltration? She guessed that was what the

colonel was calling her escape attempt. Sarah looked around the base, noticing for the first time that it seemed almost deserted. Now the majority of soldiers on guard wore the black and gold of the Special Forces. No scientists were to be seen. Clearly, Colonel Moss had taken his chance to assume full control.

"These measures are for your own protection," his announcement continued. "Please assist HIDRA Special Forces at all times and report any suspicious activity. Remember, terrorists don't wear badges – watch your co-workers. This is Colonel Moss, out."

The speakers crackled off and they reached Louise's building.

"So who are these terrorists?" Sarah asked the soldier as he opened the door for her. "What do they want?"

The soldier looked at her like she was stupid. "To get their hands on a contained sample of the virus and weaponize it. You kids are lucky to have Colonel Moss's protection."

Sarah shook her head as she walked through the door. "Yeah. Really lucky."

Louise threw her arms around Sarah as she walked into the room. *I missed you!*

Sarah stroked her hair. *Me too. Have they been looking after you?*

Louise nodded and pointed to a box in the corner. *They brought a new game, but I don't like it. That boy tried to make me play, but I wouldn't do it for him.*

What boy? Sarah asked with a frown.

The nasty one. He's tall with black hair and mean eyes.

Octavio, Sarah said.

Louise nodded. *That's him. He came before. He pretended to be nice at first, but I could tell he wasn't. Then he got angry when I wouldn't do what he said.*

Did he hurt you?

Louise shook her head, but Sarah saw her bottom lip tremble. She placed a hand on her shoulder.

It's okay, I'm back now. I won't let him upset you again. She looked at the box in the corner. *But we'd better do what they want – at least until we can find a way out of the base.*

Louise nodded and went to fetch the box. Sarah watched her open the lid and start unpacking the latest test. *If she can be brave, then so can I,* Sarah thought to herself. Moss might have killed Daniel and taken control of the base, but eventually she'd find a way to make him pay.

* * *

An hour later, as she left Louise's room, Sarah found Octavio waiting for her in the corridor outside. He gave a sneering smile as she passed. He tapped one finger to his forehead.

So, you still think you can get away, do you? Just remember that I can hear everything you say in there.

Sarah rounded on him. *Do you enjoy being Moss's little spy? Makes you feel important, does it?*

Octavio shrugged. *You seem to be doing well with Louise. Got her convinced that you're a friend? Dr. Andersen will be pleased. Just keep on reporting back and I'm sure she'll give you a reward – like some new clothes or a DVD player. Too bad it's Colonel Moss who's the real boss around here. You picked the wrong team, Sarah.*

Sarah took a step forward. *And what do you get from Colonel Moss? I'm sure it must be something more than a few computer games every month to make it worthwhile.*

The colonel has such big plans for us, Sarah, he replied. *We're all going to be soldiers in his new army. And when that happens, I'd rather be a leader than a follower, wouldn't you? I can sense how powerful you've already become. If we work together...*

He reached out to touch her arm, but Sarah knocked his hand away.

"Keep your hands off me," she said aloud, not bothering to hide the contempt in her voice.

Octavio's expression hardened. *Too bad your brother isn't developing so fast as you and Louise. Maybe I should pay him a visit too – see if I can force whatever skills he's hiding out of him.*

Sarah stepped forward and poked a finger into his chest. "Stay away from Robert and Louise. Stay away, or I promise you'll regret it."

A grin split his face. *That's more like it. We'll make a soldier out of you yet...*

Octavio! Leave her alone!

They turned to see Nestor standing in the open exit. Octavio gave an irritated sigh. He looked back at Sarah and shrugged.

Oh well, three's a crowd. See you around the dome sometime.

Not if I see you first, Sarah shot back as he swaggered down the corridor. He brushed past Nestor heavily on his way out the door.

She's out of your league, brother.

Nestor watched Octavio depart and then looked back at Sarah, red-faced.

"I'm sorry about him," he said. "He doesn't know how to behave around people any more."

Sarah gave a short laugh. "Does this good cop, bad cop routine work with all the kids here? You two are quite a team."

"What do you mean?"

Sarah walked towards him. "You're Colonel Moss's prize possessions, aren't you? Good little soldiers. Both do as you're told, right?"

Nestor shook his head. "Hey, I'm not like that. I'm not like him."

Sarah cut him short. *You're no different to them. You just go along with whatever they want.*

That's not true.

Okay, prove it.

She walked past him out of the building, where a pair of Special Forces soldiers waited to take her back to her room. As they reached the entrance to her building, Sarah looked round to see Nestor standing alone in the middle of the dome.

Their eyes met for a moment before she turned and allowed herself to be led inside.

The HIDRA truck had veered off the parallel track and driven up the side of a dune.

Daniel half staggered, half crawled to the cab and

pressed the button on the airlock entrance. The door swung open and he hauled himself into the decontamination chamber. Finally being out of the blazing sun might have made him cry with relief – except he was too dehydrated for tears.

He found the inner door release panel and pressed a button. A warning message flashed up on the screen: *Decontamination procedure not complete – override?*

"Hell yes, override!" he said hoarsely and slammed his fist onto the panel. The inner door slid open with a warning sound.

The two soldiers were slumped in their seats, both having become victims of the fall virus. Daniel crawled into the front of the truck and started rooting around the passenger seat. He found what he wanted – a half-finished bottle of water. With a gasp he unscrewed the top and took a mouthful of the life-saving liquid, being careful not to take too much at once. The last thing he wanted to do was vomit it all straight back up again.

He slumped against the wall and closed the door of the cab, allowing himself a few moments' rest. The air-con system of the truck was still working and the inner temperature regulated to a deliciously cool twenty degrees within seconds. For a moment Daniel closed his eyes, thinking how wonderful it would be just to stay like this for ever...

He slapped a hand across his face and blinked twice. "Get it together, Dan!"

He thought of Sarah and Robert still at the base – this was no time for taking a rest, even if he had crawled through the desert to get there. He finished the last of the water and hauled the driver out of his seat. As Daniel reached for the ignition, he caught sight of himself in one of the side mirrors: his burned and blistered skin, cracked lips and bloodshot eyes. He decided he'd looked better, but that was the least of his worries. They had his children and he was going to get them back.

Daniel gunned the engine and reversed the truck off the dune. Swinging the wheel round, he sent the vehicle hell for leather in the direction of the HIDRA base.

24

Rachel watched as her scientists prepped Major Bright for the experiment that would probably finish him. He stood in the middle of the laboratory, silent and impassive as the technicians attached sensors to his upper body. With that job done, they led him over to something that looked like a dentist's chair. This chair, however, was fitted with wrist and ankle restraints. Rachel saw Colonel Moss watching the preparations from the other side of the observation window and walked through the airlock to join him.

"Is that necessary?" he asked as Major Bright's arms and legs were secured.

Rachel shrugged. "It's for his protection. We don't know what's going to happen once he's injected with the modified virus."

She looked at the rack of specimens on the desk near the chair. There were six vials of liquid, each containing a different blood sample: one from each of the children on the base. Over the past twenty-four hours the samples had been filtered and treated until they contained something that would, hopefully, give Major Bright each of their powers without sending him into a fall virus coma.

Rachel sighed. If it worked, it would be a miracle. Beside her, Colonel Moss could barely contain himself, clenching and unclenching his fists with excitement.

Without warning, a siren split the air. Outside the lab, other alarms sounded simultaneously.

"That's the dome integrity alert!" one of the technicians exclaimed.

Moss grabbed his communicator with a curse. "This is Colonel Moss. Perimeter security, report now."

A harried voice crackled back on the other end. "Something hit the dome, sir! Could've been a vehicle. There's been a breach."

Moss slammed his fist down on the desk and grabbed

a breathing mask from a hook by the door.

"I'm going to check this out," he snapped. "Hold the experiment until I'm back. I want to see this."

With that, he disappeared from the lab. Rachel waited a moment before moving to follow.

"What about him?" the technician asked, jerking a thumb in the direction of Major Bright.

"You heard Colonel Moss," Rachel replied as she pulled on her breathing mask. "Hold the experiment."

She went through the airlock out of the lab. A Special Forces soldier stood on guard outside.

"What's going on here?" she asked.

"Some kind of explosion at the edge of the dome," he replied flatly. "Looks like it ripped a hole."

"Then get your breathing mask on!" Rachel exclaimed. "The air outside is still contaminated!"

She looked around the scene of chaos. Smoke rose from the north-west side of the dome and a hot desert air was blowing sand and dust through a jagged tear. Sirens wailed around the base and people ran in all directions, desperate to get to their protective suits as quickly as possible. A group of mirror-masks ran past her in the direction of the smoke, carrying tools to repair the rip. Straining to see, Rachel made out the burning wreck of a military truck near the breach – it looked like one of theirs.

Whatever was going on, Rachel's first priority was to make sure her people were safe. She ran twenty metres to the nearest security post and grabbed the intercom.

"This is Dr. Andersen," she said into the mic. Her voice boomed out of the emergency speakers all around the base. "Dome integrity has been compromised. All science personnel are to stay within sealed buildings until further notice. Breathing masks must be worn for movement around the base. This is not a drill. Repeat, this is not a drill."

She slammed the mic back into its cradle and made to run in the direction of the tear – if people were injured, they'd need her there.

"Not so fast, doctor," a man's voice hissed from behind her. She stiffened as the muzzle of a gun was pressed into her back. It was impossible to tell whether the weapon was a dart-gun or something more deadly.

"Back this way. Move quick."

A man's hand grabbed Rachel roughly and pulled her behind the cover of a nearby building. When they were out of sight, he released her arm and she turned slowly. The first thing that struck her was the appearance of her attacker: his face was dirt-smeared and badly sunburned. She thought of the hole in the dome and realized that he must have come in from the outside.

"Give me your key card," the man demanded, weapon raised. Rachel now saw he held a dart-gun – non-lethal. He followed her gaze and guessed her thoughts.

"I could stun you and then rip off your mask," he threatened hoarsely, as if he was badly in need of water. "This air is still contaminated, right?"

Rachel unclipped the key-card from her belt and tossed it. The man caught it deftly, keeping his eyes locked on her at all times. By the redness around the pupils, she judged that he was in the advanced stages of the viral infection and perhaps only had a short time before he entered a coma. If he'd been out in the desert, she wondered how he'd managed to fight off the effects of the fall virus for so long.

"I take it that's your handiwork," she said, nodding at the rising smoke from the explosion. "Do you know how many people you've put in danger? If you needed medical help, all you had to do was go to the main gate."

"I've seen the kind of medical help HIDRA gives," he said bitterly. "Where are my children?"

Rachel frowned. "What do you mean?"

"Sarah and Robert," he snapped back. "I'm taking them out of this place."

The man's identity suddenly became clear to her. "You're Daniel Williams! But you're meant to be in a coma..."

Daniel grabbed her arm again and pointed the gun in her face. "Don't play stupid with me. You're one of the head scientists, right? You run this place, so you know what goes on. It seems the colonel's idea of patient care is leaving people for dead in the desert."

Rachel shook her head. "I run the scientific operation. Colonel Moss is in control of security..."

"And you were just doing your job?" he interrupted with a harsh laugh. "He tried to have me killed."

"I didn't know anything about that, believe me. Colonel Moss is out of control."

Daniel loosened his grip a little. "What have you been doing with my children?"

Rachel pulled free of his grasp. "I've been protecting them!"

Daniel shook his head. "You're just as much a part of this as—"

"FREEZE!"

They both looked round. The Special Forces soldier from outside the lab stood a few metres away. He had an automatic pistol aimed at Daniel's head.

"Drop the weapon," the soldier ordered. "I *will* shoot you."

Daniel's shoulders slumped. He handed the dart-gun to Rachel with a final, accusatory glance.

"Looks like you helped catch the intruder, doctor," the soldier said, moving forward with the gun still raised. "Colonel Moss will be pleased."

Daniel laughed humourlessly. "Yes, well done. You should feel proud of yourself."

"Hit the ground," the soldier barked. "Hands on your head."

Daniel lay face down as the soldier advanced. Rachel stepped back, weighing the dart-gun in her hand.

"Are you okay, Dr. Andersen?" the soldier asked as he put his boot on Daniel's back and reached for a set of wrist restraints on his belt. "Did he hurt you?"

"Not as much as this will," Rachel answered. She raised the dart-gun and shot the soldier in the neck. His body stiffened and his hand shot up to the embedded dart. A second later he toppled heavily over and landed face-first on the ground.

Daniel turned his head and looked at her. "Changing sides, doctor?"

Rachel shrugged. "I've exhausted my diplomatic efforts with the colonel."

Daniel pushed the unconscious soldier to one side and got to his feet. Rachel offered him the dart-gun but he picked up the automatic instead.

"This will be more persuasive," he said, sticking the

weapon in his belt. "Where's Sarah being kept?"

"In one of the observation cells," Rachel replied. "Colonel Moss is keeping her prisoner with the other kids."

Daniel's eyes flashed anger, but he said nothing. He snatched the wrist restraints from the fallen soldier. "Let's stash this guy before he comes round."

"There's a storeroom where we can hide him," Rachel suggested, "but you might want to grab his uniform first. And wash your face. You stand out a bit at the moment."

He nodded. "Good idea. Thanks for sticking your neck out."

"Colonel Moss has been having it all his own way for too long," Rachel replied. "It's time someone stood up to him."

Daniel grinned. "Then let's do it."

Sarah ignored the soldier as he entered the room and walked round the side of her bed.

"I'm not going anywhere with you," she said firmly from where she lay, keeping her eyes locked on the ceiling. "I'm not doing what Moss wants until I've seen Robert. If you try to get me out of this bed, I'll scream."

The soldier towered over her with his back to the mirror.

"I see you're as friendly as ever," he said quietly.

Sarah looked round at him in disbelief. "Dan—!"

She stopped herself as Daniel shook his head slightly and jerked a thumb in the direction of the mirror. Mandy would be listening in.

"I'm taking you to the colonel," he said as he began to unhook the restraints holding her in place. "No more arguments."

"Okay, fine," Sarah said aloud, moving to a sitting position so she could whisper to him. "I thought you were dead!"

Daniel shook his head. "It'll take more than a short walk through the desert to finish me. But my doctor tells me I might not have long before the fall virus really takes hold, so we'd better move fast."

"You there," Mandy's voice crackled through the speaker. "Who gave you authorization to take this patient?"

Daniel looked back at the mirror.

"Colonel Moss wants to conduct more tests on her," he said, trying to sound as official as possible.

"I didn't receive that order."

"Well he's kinda busy with the security breach right now..." Daniel began.

Mandy cut him short. "Stay there. I'm calling through for confirm—"

There was a hissing sound through the speaker, as if a sleep dart had been fired near the mic, followed by a thud. Daniel and Sarah looked at one another.

"Mandy's taking a nap," Rachel said from the mirror. "Well, don't just stand there! Get moving!"

Sarah didn't need telling twice. She jumped out of the bed and dressed in seconds while Daniel watched the door. Rachel joined them as they ran for the exit.

"I have to get back to Colonel Moss," she told them as they scanned the dome. "I'll try to keep him distracted for as long as possible. Robert's being kept over there." She motioned to one of the other buildings. "We probably have about an hour before Mandy and that soldier wake up. After that, I'll try to hold things up as much as possible while you escape. Good luck."

She walked down the ramp, but Sarah ran after her, catching her arm.

"Thank you," Sarah said as she threw her arms around her. "Come with us."

"I have to stay for my scientists," Rachel said, pulling away. "Colonel Moss is going to go crazy when he finds out I helped you, but I can't just run away."

"It isn't going to be safe for you here," Daniel said.

Rachel shrugged. "Even the colonel would think twice about harming a high-ranking scientist – I hope." Her voice trailed away, not sounding very convinced. Then she said with resolve, "Just get out of here and tell the world what Colonel Moss is doing. We're about three hours' drive from the edge of the quarantine zone, but there are HIDRA checkpoints set up on all roads leading out. The colonel probably has men loyal to him stationed on all of them."

"We'll cross that bridge when we come to it," Daniel answered. "First we have to make it out of the base."

Rachel nodded and wished them luck once more. Sarah watched her walk away and then turned to Daniel, a wave of concern washing over her as she saw him leaning against the side of the building, his face full of fatigue.

"Are you okay?"

Daniel nodded and pushed himself up. "For now. What's the plan?"

Sarah bit her lip.

"You get us a vehicle," she said, looking at the airlock in the distance. "I'll get Robert. I'll need some help breaking into his cell."

Daniel frowned. "What are you going to do?"

"I'm going to pick up a friend."

25

When Rachel returned to the lab, she found Colonel Moss already there and standing in front of the observation window. As she entered, he turned and fixed her with a cold stare.

"Is everything okay?" she asked, trying to keep her voice calm.

"My men have the situation under control," he snapped. "The breach is being stabilized. Where have you been?"

"I needed to check some of the sleeper caskets before

transportation," she replied, casting an eye over the monitoring equipment. "You wouldn't want any of the patients dying in transit, would you?"

Colonel Moss gave her a cold smile that told her he really didn't give a damn. In her absence he'd ordered the scientists to begin the experiment without her. *Impatient as ever*, Rachel thought. *The fool.*

"From now on I want you close," he said, keeping his eyes locked on Bright. "Just in case there are complications."

Rachel sighed. "You're injecting one of your men with something we haven't even properly tested on lab rats, Colonel. Of course there are going to be complications."

She beckoned over the nearest lab technician.

"What's Major Bright's status?" she asked.

"We injected the first modified viral sample five minutes ago," the man responded. "His heart-rate went through the roof. We thought we were going to lose him, but he pulled through. Somehow."

Rachel stared at Major Bright through the glass as he strained against the wrist bonds holding his arms in place. His eyes were wide and bloodshot. She hadn't thought it possible, but he actually looked madder and meaner than normal.

"Of course he pulled through," Colonel Moss snapped.

"He's ex-SAS. Now inject him with the virus farmed from Octavio."

Rachel turned to face Moss.

"Colonel, this is madness," she pleaded. "We don't know what—"

Moss held up a hand to silence her.

"I've been patient for two years. Now I need results. You'll inject Major Bright with another sample or you'll take his place in the chair, Dr. Andersen."

Rachel sighed and looked round at the technician.

"Do it," she ordered. "If he survives that, give him the other four samples. The colonel wants results."

Moss nodded with approval and tapped the glass like someone trying to get the attention of an animal at the zoo. Major Bright's head jerked round at the sound. His eyes glared at them as if he didn't really know what he was seeing.

"Well done, Rachel," said Colonel Moss. "I knew you wouldn't let me down."

"Sarah!" Louise cried as the soldier showed her through into the room. "You've already been today."

Sarah motioned for her to sit on the bed and grabbed the *Monopoly* board from the side.

"Aww, not that again," Louise moaned, flouncing her arms. "I'm bored. I don't like this game. I don't like any of the games they gave us. I want to go outside."

"Come on," Sarah cajoled. "You know they won't let us do that. Play with me..."

Just pretend you're having fun, she told the younger girl. *We're getting out of here now. I need you to help us.*

Louise nodded, her mouth open a little as she started to help Sarah set up the paper money in the tray.

"I didn't know you were coming again today, Sarah," Magda said from the mirror. "Who brought you over?"

From the corner of her eye, Sarah saw the green light on the door handle turn red. Magda had just locked them in.

"They let me come by myself," Sarah replied, not looking round. "As a reward for good behaviour."

Magda laughed. "From what I've heard, you haven't been behaving well at all..."

Sarah shut out her voice and concentrated on Louise.

I want you to do something for me.

What is it, Sarah?

Do you think you can try to break the mirror again?

The younger girl frowned and shook her head. *But I was told not to...*

You want to get out, don't you?

But Magda will be angry…

It's okay. Nobody's going to tell you off. Do it for me, okay?

Louise looked uncertain for a moment, but then nodded. She walked over to the mirror and closed her eyes. For a few seconds nothing happened. She looked back at Sarah.

I can't...

An alarm sounded in the dome outside. Louise's eyes widened with fear as she heard it.

"What's happening out there?" Louise asked. "Those alarms have been going off all day."

"It's okay," Sarah said, moving over to place a hand on the younger girl's shoulder. She directed her mind beyond the walls of the room, out into the area under the dome. Already damaged by Daniel's entrance, the dome had begun to sag and tear even further – it looked like the whole thing was going to come down any minute.

"Sarah, I want you and Louise to sit down on the bed," Magda ordered with a distinct edge in her voice.

Sensing that time was running out, Sarah grabbed Louise by the shoulders and turned her round, perhaps a little too roughly.

You can break the mirror, Louise! YOU MUST!

Sarah stopped as she saw the girl's eyes begin to fill

with tears. She put her arms around her.

I'm sorry. I'm sorry. I didn't mean to shout...

"Sarah, are you listening to me?" Magda demanded again.

The younger girl let out a sob and pulled away from Sarah's embrace. Wiping away the tears from her eyes, she looked back at the mirror with a frown.

"Louise, be a good girl and sit down on your bed," Magda ordered. "I'm sending in the guard."

I don't want to stay here any more! Louise's mind screamed out.

She held out her hand at the mirror, fingers splayed. The image in the glass distorted strangely, like a funhouse reflection. The centre began to push inwards as if some unseen force was pressing on it. A crack began in the top right corner and grew towards the middle. Another appeared in the bottom left.

"Stop that!" Magda ordered, a note of panic in her voice. "Step away from the glass! Sarah, make her stop!"

But it was too late for that. With a mighty crack, the mirror exploded into the other room, leaving a gaping hole. On the other side of the gap Magda sheltered in the corner, showered with shards of broken glass. Sarah looked at Louise, first in surprise and then with a spreading grin. She threw her arms around her again.

You did it!

There wasn't a moment to lose. Rising, Sarah jumped through the hole and pulled Louise after her.

"Stay where you are!" Magda cried. Sarah sensed she was afraid of them. *Good.*

"Hello, Magda," said Sarah, taking a step forward. "I'm leaving now and Louise is coming with me."

Magda brushed pieces of mirror off her coat and stood up. She produced an electric stun gun from her pocket and levelled it at Sarah. "I want you to go back into the room, Sarah. There's an emergency in the base and it's not safe. Being shocked by this thing isn't a nice experience. Come one step closer and I'll hit you with it twice."

Sarah put up her hands and backed away, but her thoughts went out to the woman.

A wave of images swept through Sarah's mind. Visions of things that she had never seen before: a family, holidays at the beach, birthdays, driving a car, swimming in the ocean. She went on looking for anything that could be useful to her. It was just like watching TV, flipping between memories like changing channels. Sarah zeroed in on a series of images. Snakes. Fear. Flight.

Magda had a phobia of snakes. Sarah grinned a little as she began to visualize a long, black snake sliding up the woman's arm. Then she sent the image to Magda's brain...

Magda's eyes widened as she looked down at her wrist. Her lips screamed help but no sound escaped. She clawed frantically at the snake that was winding itself around her arm, invisible to everyone but her. The stun gun clattered to the ground as she pressed herself into the corner of the room, sobbing quietly. Sarah took Louise's hand and led her to the door, keeping her eyes on the woman.

"Unlock the door, Magda," she said quietly. "And don't try to chase us. You know what we can do."

With a whimper, Magda reached for a switch in her control room and the red light by the door went green. They ran into the corridor, slamming the door behind them. The woman didn't follow.

"We have to get my brother," Sarah said, squeezing Louise's hand. "Then we can get out of here. Think you can do your trick with the mirror again?"

Louise nodded seriously, but resisted when Sarah pulled her towards the outer door of the building.

"I want to get Wei first," she said. "He's my friend."

Sarah almost argued, but saw the determination in the other girl's eyes.

Okay. Let's get them both.

26

The HIDRA base was caught up in a flurry of activity that bordered on chaos. Soldiers and scientists ran all around, too preoccupied with securing the dome once more to notice two kids out by themselves.

Clutching each other's hands tightly, Sarah and Louise ran across the dome to a building that stood near the parked helicopter. They ran up the ramp, looking out for guards as they went. Next to the entrance door, Sarah noticed a printed sign: *Test Subject 6 – Sikong Wei*.

Inside, they found the door of the observation room

standing open and the room beyond deserted. On the other side of the two-way glass a boy of Robert's age stood in the centre of his cell. His jet black hair framed delicate, Chinese features and intelligent eyes. He looked at the mirror expectantly.

Stand back! Sarah ordered the boy and he stepped away.

Louise held up her hand and frowned with concentration. This time the mirror started to warp and crack within a few seconds, exploding into the room away from them. *She's getting stronger*, thought Sarah.

"I knew you were coming!" the kid cried as he jumped through the open window into the room. His English was perfect, his Chinese accent the only indication that it wasn't his first language. *Nice to finally meet you, Louise!*

Sarah cut their greeting short, grabbing Louise's hand again and pulling her back towards the door.

"Nice to meet you too, Wei," Louise called back. "But we've got to get Robert. He's on the other side of the dome."

Outside, however, a group of mirror-masked soldiers were deploying, seemingly unconcerned by the crisis. They wore Special Forces colours on their suits and were clearly on the lookout for them.

They know we've escaped! Louise thought, starting to sound frightened. *Magda must have told them!*

Sarah shook her head, looking at the open space they had to cross to get to where Robert was being kept. *We'll never make it.*

I can help, Wei sent to them. *Let's make a distraction...*

He took a half step forward and placed his hands against his temple, brow furrowed with concentration. Sarah looked at Louise questioningly, who placed a hand on Sarah's lower arm.

Stand back, she warned.

Wei closed his eyes even tighter as a spark of fire appeared before him and shot forward across the plastic covering on the floor. The line of flame – no more than a foot high, but burning intensely – streaked towards the group of soldiers. One of them turned – too late to avoid the fire. The soldier leaped back and started rolling on the floor as flames shot up the side of his suit. The others turned at the sound of his cries and frantically began patting at him with their gloves.

Sarah didn't waste any time. "Come on," she said, grabbing Louise's hand and dragging her in the direction of Robert's building. Wei opened his eyes and followed them.

They crossed the dome quickly, overlooked by the mirror-masks – they were too busy trying to put out the blaze that was burning through the plastic flooring. Sarah looked at Wei and patted him on the shoulder.

Thanks, she said. *You're a handy guy to have around.*

Well done, Wei! Louise beamed at him.

The kid shrugged. *Just something I've been practising.*

Looking round the side of the building, Sarah saw their next problem. Two masked soldiers with dart-guns stood guard at the doorway. They must have expected her to come back for Robert. She remembered the trick with the snake she'd played on Mandy, but doubted she could do it on two people at once.

It's no good, she thought, turning back to the others. *They've got the door covered. I can't leave without Robert.*

Louise moved round to face the wall they were standing near.

Stand back, she ordered. *I think I can do this...*

Frowning with concentration, she held out a hand at the wall. The metal began to groan and buckle inwards with a tearing sound. Sarah and Wei leaped back, just in time. A second later a hole ripped through the steel, revealing the room beyond. Robert stood on the other side, blinking at them with amazement.

"Don't just stand there, jump!" Sarah ordered, holding out her arms to him.

Without a second thought, her brother flew through the gap, landing heavily against her. She hugged him for a moment, but they didn't have time to waste.

Now let's get out of here! she commanded the others, taking charge. *We're going out through the tear.*

They ran round the side of the building, making for the exit that had been torn in the dome. It was then that a mirror-mask stepped out, blocking their way. They pulled up sharply. Louise let out a cry as the man raised the dart-gun in his hands. He pulled the trigger.

The tiny dart flew silently through the air, embedding itself in Wei's arm. The boy looked round at it stupidly for a moment, before his eyes rolled up in his head and he fell back onto the ground. Sarah kneeled by his side and pulled the missile out of his arm. The mirror-mask calmly levelled the dart-gun at her for another shot.

It didn't come.

Instead, their attacker's legs buckled and he crashed to the ground, the dart-gun skittering to Sarah's feet. Daniel stood above the fallen mirror-mask, a pistol clutched in his hand.

Sarah thought she'd never been so glad to see anyone in her life. Robert let out a cry, running to throw his arms around him. "Daniel, you're okay!"

"Sorry I took so long," Daniel said, ruffling Robert's hair. "I found another truck. Let's go."

The danger signal went off in Sarah's head as she was about to reply. She snatched the dart-gun from the ground, spun round and fired twice. Two mirror-masks crashed to the floor before her, darts sticking through their suits.

"Nice reflexes!" exclaimed Daniel.

Sarah handed him the dart-gun. "A lot's happened since we saw you last."

"Tell me about it on the road," he replied, picking up the sleeping body of Wei in his arms.

They made for the exit at a run, skirting around the edge of the wall to avoid being seen. Amazingly, they almost made it to the gap without being noticed.

Almost.

A figure appeared as they reached the tear in the dome. The dust blowing in from the desert parted for him as he walked.

Octavio.

On seeing Sarah he smiled and shook his head. *You didn't really think that you'd make it out of here, did you?*

Daniel looked at her in confusion. "Another friend of yours?"

"You can come with us," Sarah said. "Either that, or get out of our way."

Octavio grinned nastily. "No way. Colonel Moss ordered me to keep tabs on you. Looks like he's going to be very pleased with me."

Daniel stepped forward, holding up the dart-gun.

"Look, kid, we're kind of in a hurry here so..."

"Daniel—" Sarah warned too late.

Octavio threw out his right hand. An invisible force hit Daniel like a sledgehammer, driving him backwards on the ground. Wei and the dart-gun went flying from his arms.

Sarah rounded on Octavio, concentrating on his thoughts, feeling his anger, looking for something she could use against him.

Get out of my head! he screamed and the force hit her hard, almost knocking her down. *You're all going to do as I say!*

"Octavio, that's enough!"

Nestor appeared through the smoke. Daniel looked round at Sarah as he struggled to his feet, rubbing his arm.

"What the hell is this, Sarah?" he asked.

"Sibling rivalry," she replied, looking at Nestor. He seemed taller than before, more resolved as he faced his brother.

"I'm going with them, Octavio," he said calmly. "It's no good here. Colonel Moss isn't our friend. He just gives us lots of stuff to keep us quiet. To make us do what he wants."

Octavio shook his head. *You can't fight me, Nestor,* he said with a laugh. *You know I always beat you.*

But can you beat us all at once? Nestor asked. He moved to stand near Sarah and Louise. Robert stood forward also. A look of doubt flickered across Octavio's face.

You can't leave...

Come with us...

Octavio shook his head violently, holding out a hand at his brother. Nestor staggered back, hit by the strength of Octavio's telekinetic power, but he kept his feet. Now he raised his hands and a wind rose, its power directed towards Octavio. All around, the temperature dropped. Suddenly a storm was raging about them.

Octavio struggled to keep his feet and snarled at his brother, *I've been waiting for an excuse to do this.*

He redirected his power at Nestor and hit him with another wall of telekinetic energy. Nestor held up his hands to drive back the force, but it was too late. He staggered back and lost his footing. A line of blood trickled from his nose, as if he had been smashed in the face. He wiped it away with a trembling hand. Sarah tried to move to help him, but found herself held in place.

Octavio had overlooked Louise, however. She calmly looked at the sagging roof above them and pointed a single finger upwards...

Something overhead cracked violently and one of the metal girders supporting the dome crashed to the ground centimetres from Octavio. Immediately the force he was directing at them subsided as a second girder came down, bringing with it a chunk of the dome covering.

Daniel picked up Wei and started running for the hole in the wall, ignoring the billowing dust. "Come on!" he yelled.

Sarah and Robert pulled Nestor to his feet and dragged him away, while Louise ran after them. They followed Daniel out into the night, not waiting to see if Octavio or Colonel Moss's men were following. Above them, a huge section of the dome roof tore and fell…

Sarah only stopped to look back when they'd reached the HIDRA truck Daniel had stolen. A quarter of the dome appeared to have collapsed, temporarily blocking off the hole they'd come through. A mirror-mask had chased them out, but quickly turned back when he realized he was outnumbered.

"Octavio," Nestor said, looking back at the collapsing dome. He made to return, but Sarah held his arm firm.

"He's okay," she said. "Can't you sense it?"

Nestor nodded and allowed himself to be pulled into the vehicle.

"Let's get out of here!" Daniel cried. He bundled the unconscious Wei into the truck and jumped behind the wheel. The others piled in. "And buckle up. It's going to be bumpy!"

"Where are we going?" Sarah asked as he threw the truck round in a circle that sent it bouncing over the dunes, jolting them in their seats. The cab of the truck was spacious and packed with scientific equipment and boxes of supplies.

"East, out of the HIDRA quarantine zone," Daniel shouted above the noise of the engine. "If we can make it that far, we can go hell for leather to Melbourne and tell the authorities what's going on. What is going on, by the way? I feel like I've missed all of the action."

"It's a long story," Sarah replied.

She looked back at the others, strapped into their seats. Louise and Robert looked scared. Wei still slept.

Nestor looked out at the night sky through one of the windows.

"I'm glad you're back," she said quietly. "Thank you, Daniel."

"I said I wouldn't leave you," he replied, not taking his eyes from the narrow dirt track they were following. "But there's just one thing..."

Sarah noticed that his voice sounded suddenly very weary, as if he had expended all his energy on the rescue. Looking at Daniel, Sarah saw his eyelids hanging heavy and when he looked at her he seemed to be fighting hard just to keep them open. The virus.

"Oh, no..."

He gave her a weak smile.

"The doc said I wouldn't have much time. Any of you guys know how to drive a truck?"

27

The interior of the HIDRA truck looked a bit like a mobile home, with two seats up front for the driver and passenger and a big open space in the rear with seating and fold-down beds set into the walls. The back was packed with all sorts of scientific equipment, and was clearly designed for research expeditions. Robert and Louise waited in the rear with the sleeping Wei while the older members of the group crowded round the front. The dashboard of the truck was a confusing array of switches and computer read-outs, but Daniel assured

Nestor that he didn't have to use most of them. It was much bigger than a normal vehicle, but the principles of driving it were the same.

"This is the brake," Daniel told him, pointing to the pedal in the middle at his feet. "The clutch is used when you change the gears. That's the accelerator. You steer with the wheel."

"Thanks, he's not totally stupid," Sarah said, punching Daniel in the arm.

Daniel laughed, but she could sense the fatigue spreading through him. He didn't have long before the virus took hold fully. He motioned for Nestor to sit in the driver's seat. The boy was tall for his age and his feet easily reached the pedals.

"The important thing to remember is to put the clutch down when you want to change gears," Daniel instructed, pointing to the pedal on the left.

"Why would I want to change gears?" Nestor asked.

"You change up gears when you want to go faster. Or change down to a lower gear if you're going up a steep dune or hill. And you have to take your foot off the clutch and push down on the accelerator smoothly, or you'll stall the engine."

Sarah looked out of the windscreen at the darkened

desert in front of the truck. They'd parked by the side of the track and turned off the exterior lights in case their pursuers saw them in the distance. Every second they sat there brought Colonel Moss's men closer. Sarah knew as soon as they repaired the dome, they'd be following.

"Why did they make it so difficult to use?" Nestor asked irritably, taking the massive wheel in his hands. "It's impossible."

Daniel looked to Sarah for some support.

"Nestor, there's no other choice," she said, laying a hand on the boy's shoulder. "I know you can do this."

Nestor met her eyes and nodded, seeming to take strength from her encouragement. He reached round and turned the key in the ignition. The truck's engine sprang into noisy life.

"Give it a try," Daniel said. "Just take it slow, kid."

Gripping the wheel more firmly, Nestor put his foot down on the clutch like Daniel had shown and pushed the gear stick forward into first. There was a horrible grinding sound as he did it.

"Gently!" Daniel ordered as Nestor began to take his foot off the clutch and step on the accelerator. The truck lurched forward violently and the wheel jerked in his hand, completely out of control. A second later the engine cut out completely.

Nestor looked round at the others apologetically. "I'm sorry I just..."

He stopped short as he saw Daniel leaning against the driver's seat just to keep on his feet. Sarah leaped to his side.

"Robert, help me!" she cried, grabbing Daniel's arm. Together they dragged him to the back of the cab. Louise unfolded a bed from the wall and they laid him down.

"Thanks," Daniel said weakly. "I'm sorry."

Sarah looked round at Robert. "Help Nestor get this thing moving."

Her brother nodded and moved to the front of the truck. Louise handed Sarah a bottle of water which she placed against Daniel's lips. He managed a few sips before having to lay back.

"Try to drink some more," Sarah said. "You're badly dehydrated."

Daniel shook his head and pushed the bottle away. He reached inside his shirt and removed something. "I have to give you this…"

"Daniel..." Sarah began to protest, but fell silent when she saw what he was offering her – the bag of diamonds.

"Colonel Moss was kind enough to leave these on me," he said, his voice little more than a whisper. "You have to take them now. They're worth over two million dollars – enough for you and Robert to manage without me for as long as you need to."

Sarah opened the bag and looked at the precious contents. Inside was also a mobile phone sim card.

"My contact in Melbourne is called Alexei," Daniel explained. "His number's on the card."

Sarah shook her head and tried to hand him back the bag. "I can't do this..."

"You can and you will, Sarah," he said.

"But they're stolen," she protested.

"Stolen from criminals who didn't own them in the first place," Daniel assured her. "No one of any worth will miss them. You're stronger than all of us. Just get this truck out of here. Keep heading to Melbourne..."

His eyes began to close.

"Dad!" she cried. It was the first time she'd called him that in eight years and the word seemed to bring him back momentarily.

He smiled as Robert rushed to her side. "You two have to look after yourselves now. Take those diamonds and start a new life. *Do some good with them...*"

His voice trailed away and he was gone into a sleep he wouldn't be waking from any time soon. Silence fell in the truck.

Finally, Sarah stepped back, aware of them all looking at her. Daniel was gone – she took a deep breath and wiped a tear from her eye.

"Put your seat belts on," she ordered. "We've got to get moving again. Are you ready, Nestor?"

In the driver's seat, the Colombian boy nodded. Robert started strapping Daniel in place in the bed while the others took their seats. Sarah gave his shoulder a squeeze.

He's going to be okay. We'll find a cure.

Robert nodded silently as Sarah moved to sit at Nestor's side. Taking a deep breath, he turned the key in the ignition once more and the massive engine roared into life. This time Nestor found the balance between the clutch and the accelerator as the truck moved forwards. The uneven road caused the wheel to jerk first right and then left as the vehicle picked up speed. He almost stalled again when he changed gears so he decided to leave it in second, even though it meant that the truck was crawling along at a fraction of the pace they'd made with Daniel in control. At least they were on their way.

Good work! Sarah encouraged. *Just keep us moving...*

* * *

The desert seemed to stretch on for ever and they travelled another hour before the sandy track turned unexpectedly into a tarmac road. This made the going considerably easier. Although he was clearly exhausted, Nestor pushed the truck onwards. Sarah felt a wave of fatigue spread over her and she had to struggle to keep her own eyes open.

Eventually the truck crawled past the first buildings of a town located on the edge of the desert. The headlamps illuminated a sign on the side of the road.

"Esperinka," Nestor read as they passed the sign, peering through the windscreen.

"Population 2150," Sarah added as they moved up the high street.

Nestor pulled the vehicle to a halt. The shops that lined the streets were in complete darkness and there was no evidence of life.

"Then where is everyone?" Robert asked.

Nestor shrugged and turned off the engine, thankful to have some kind of a break from the driving.

"Probably all evacuated," he said, easing himself out of the driver's seat and moving back to lie on one of the fold-down beds that lined the side of the cab. "Or maybe they're hiding, afraid. They might think we're HIDRA."

"Yeah," added Robert. "We're driving one of their trucks."

Sarah slumped in her seat. Exhaustion swept over her. Towards the rear of the truck she saw that Wei was awake and sitting up while Louise gave him a sip of water from a bottle. Somehow they'd made it out of the base, but how far they'd managed to travel was unclear in the night. It could have been fifty kilometres or only twenty. She looked round to ask Nestor, but saw that he was already deep in sleep.

Her eyes closed involuntarily for a second and she had to fight to stay awake once more, trying to push herself up off the chair. She knew she couldn't afford to sleep. They had to get further away...

Someone placed a blanket over her as she lay on the chair. She tried to protest.

It's okay, Sarah. You rest and we'll keep watch...

It was Robert's voice in her head. She could hear the concern in his tone.

Finally, too tired to argue, she gave in and slept.

28

Rachel stood in the centre of the dome and watched her engineering team trying to shore up the fallen section. Work was progressing quickly and she estimated the dome would be secure again within the hour. She looked in the direction of the building that had housed Sarah and thought of Mandy lying asleep at her station. She wondered how much longer she had before Colonel Moss's spy woke up and raised the alarm.

A warning siren seemed to answer her question, except it came from the direction of the lab. *What now?*

It was the building containing Major Bright. She set off towards the sound of the siren at a run.

When Rachel reached the lab, she found that most of it was gone. The observation window had been broken and the equipment smashed. The dentist's chair was nowhere to be seen and the back wall was missing, as were the other scientists who had been assisting with the experiment. Rachel hoped they'd made it to safety before the lab was damaged, but she had a bad feeling not much had escaped the destruction. Colonel Moss stood in the entrance, looking at Major Bright, who was motionless in the centre of the room, staring straight ahead, a strange half-smile on his face.

Colonel Moss grabbed her arm as she entered.

"He destroyed the lab!" he hissed, pulling her close. "He looks weird."

Rachel freed herself from his grip and took a cautious step into the ruined laboratory.

"Major Bright, can you hear me?" she asked, eyeing the nearest exit as she did so – she knew there was no predicting what was going to happen next.

Bright's eyes snapped into focus and he turned to face her. Rachel had the strangest feeling that he was seeing straight into her thoughts. It wasn't a nice sensation.

"You were with them..." he said softly. "I can see it...

You helped Daniel Williams and the children escape… You've drugged two of our people…"

Rachel backed away as Colonel Moss stepped into the room.

"Well, it looks like it's going to be a whole lot harder to keep secrets from now on, Dr. Andersen," he said with grim satisfaction. He beckoned over two of his soldiers. "Put her in a cell. I'll question her later."

"Major Bright is unstable," she protested as the soldiers grabbed her arms. "You can't control him Colonel…"

"Get this traitor out of my sight," Moss spat in response.

As Rachel was led away, Colonel Moss turned back to Major Bright.

"Where are they?" he demanded. "Can you see them?"

Bright closed his eyes and swayed on the spot for a moment.

"To the east," he said finally. "Less than forty klicks. Hiding in a town."

A grin split Colonel Moss's face for the first time in days.

"How do you feel, Major?" he asked.

Bright opened his eyes and stared into the distance.

"Like I could take on the world, Colonel."

* * *

They'd come to a ghost town.

If Esperinka ever really had a population of 2150, it was gone now. Every building, every shop was deserted. The doors of businesses on the high street stood open, as if the people had left before they had time to lock up.

"Where do you think everyone went?" Sarah asked as she stood next to Nestor in the middle of the road, looking around the spookily quiet scene.

"Maybe they were evacuated," he replied, sounding unconvinced. "Or..."

"Or what?" Sarah pressed as his voice trailed away. Robert appeared from the truck and started running up and down the street, peering in shop windows.

Thousands of sleepers have passed through the HIDRA base since the meteorite hit, Nestor replied, directing his thoughts to Sarah alone, mainly so Robert couldn't hear. *But there were too many even for Moss's men to handle. I've seen sleepers packed into huge storage crates, like large versions of the caskets. I've seen the inside of one of those crates. It's scary. People kept in racks like tins of food. Waiting to be relocated by Moss.*

Sarah felt a shiver run down her spine, despite the warmth of the day. She thought about Daniel, lying asleep in the truck. She wouldn't let HIDRA put him in storage like a piece of meat.

"We should get out of here," she said, walking back to the truck.

Using the vehicle's onboard GPS system, she managed to work out that they were still about sixty kilometres west of the border with Victoria – the neighbouring state. The edge of the quarantine zone was marked there as a thick red line across the map. It didn't look too far, but they were still in the HIDRA-controlled area. She turned on the radio and found static on every station save one: a recorded message that played over and over again.

"You are in a quarantine zone. If it is safe to do so, make your way to the nearest HIDRA checkpoint for aid and medical assistance. Otherwise, stay in your home and await evacuation. For your own safety, do not try to leave the quarantine zone. Repeat, do not leave the quarantine zone. This is an official HIDRA broadcast. You are in a quarantine zone..."

She turned off the radio.

"Hey, do you hear that?" Robert cried, running over and pointing up the high street.

Nestor and Sarah listened carefully. A low humming sound grew from the north. A helicopter approaching.

Quick, get in the truck! Sarah ordered the others. *Nestor, get us moving!*

Nestor checked they had Louise and Wei on board before jumping into the driver's seat. He turned the key and pumped the accelerator. The engine turned over once, sending a judder through the truck. Then it died. Nestor turned the key again and again with the same result.

Robert stuck his head out of the open door of the cab.

"It's getting closer!" he cried. "They're looking for us!"

"Yes, I know!" Nestor replied through gritted teeth as he tried firing the engine once more. He looked round at Sarah. "What are we going to do?"

Sarah scanned the deserted high street through the windscreen. The road was built on a slight incline. Reaching down, she released the handbrake of the truck.

The massive machine began to roll forward, ever so slowly.

"We're going to drive out of here," she told Nestor, pointing ahead down the street. "But first we've got to get moving. You'll have to get out and push, all of you."

Nestor nodded, grasping her plan immediately. He jumped out of the driver's seat and ushered the others out onto the street while Sarah took his place at the wheel.

I hope you know what you're doing, he said as he went through the door and ran to the back of the truck.

So do I, Sarah thought back.

Even with the four others pushing, the truck made painfully slow progress down the street for almost a minute. Sarah wished that Daniel was awake to put a little muscle into the effort. But then they hit the part of the road which sloped downwards more steeply.

Now the truck moved quicker, generating more speed as its own weight began to add to the forward momentum. The numbers on the speedometer began to tick upwards. Sarah turned the key again. The engine turned over, threatening to spring into life this time. Then it spluttered and died. Sarah slammed her fist onto the wheel.

"Where are we going?" shouted Wei, who was running closest to the cab door.

"I'll tell you when we get there!" Sarah shouted back, a little irritably. Her sixth sense began to send her a mental image of the impending danger: a sleek, black helicopter moving through the sky in their direction. In the cockpit, two sets of eyes scanned the countryside for them.

The truck was really moving now, so she tried starting the engine again, with the same result. Through the windscreen she saw that they were fast running out of shops. The end of the high street was basically the end of the town. Once they were out in the open they would be even easier for the searchers to spot. A new idea occurred to her.

Sarah scanned the last few buildings lining the street as they approached. A dentist's office. A grocery store. A florist's with a large, open window at the front. Perfect.

Watch out! she sent to the others urgently. *Get away from the truck!*

Sensing them scatter, Sarah turned the wheel hard to the right, sending the truck on a collision course with the glass front of the florist. The vehicle mounted the pavement and smashed through the window, ploughing into the building, scattering tables and shelves in its path. She slammed on the brakes at the last possible second to avoid hitting the back wall of the shop.

"Wow!" cried Robert from the smashed front of the shop as Sarah jumped out of the cab. "That was mad!"

"Don't just stand there, get inside!" she ordered the others.

They piled into the shop, stepping over broken glass, wood and bricks. Something in the roof groaned and Sarah looked up, worrying that the damage she'd caused with the truck might cause a collapse. Thankfully, the noise stopped and the building held up.

Nestor ran to the front of the shop. He reached up to the top of the window and pulled down a metal roller screen. It came down stiffly, but got stuck halfway.

Help me!

All of them ran to the screen, pulling down on the bottom. With a screech of metal, it went down fully. The interior of the building was thrown into a half-darkness relieved only by rays of light streaming in through slits in the metal. Sarah put her face close to one of the gaps, looking out onto the high street and motioning for the others to be quiet as she did so.

For a moment the high street was silent.

Then a strong gust of wind sent dust and dead leaves flying along the pavements in its wake. The buzzing of the helicopter engine grew louder, causing the whole screen to vibrate.

The machine appeared, flying up the street alarmingly close to the ground. It was smaller than Sarah had expected, but she saw machine guns mounted on either side of the cockpit. The helicopter was only large enough to seat two and she made out a pair of mirror-masks scanning the town. The masks they wore were the same, but she noted that their suits seemed slimmer, more lightweight than those she had seen at the base. Combat models.

Sarah became aware of Louise standing at her side, staring intently through one of the slats at the machine. She started to raise her hand with the same intense look on her face she'd had when she broke the mirrors at the HIDRA base.

Louise, what are you doing? Sarah demanded, placing a hand on her arm.

I can stop them, she replied, eyes fixed on the helicopter. *I can make it crash. I feel it.*

No, Sarah ordered. *More of them will come. Besides, do you really want to hurt the people in that machine?*

When Louise looked round at her, Sarah saw tears in her eyes.

They said they could make my dad better, she explained, throwing her arms around Sarah. *But they took him away somewhere. They just wanted to get my power.*

Sarah stroked a hand through her hair and gave her shoulder a squeeze. She felt the anger coursing through the younger girl. It almost scared her.

It's okay, we'll get to the city and find your dad, Sarah told her. *I promise.*

Louise thought about this for a moment and once again Sarah could sense the turmoil in her mind. Finally,

Louise nodded and rubbed away the tears.

Okay, Sarah.

Sarah smiled and turned her attention back to the screen.

The droning sound of another helicopter joined the first and a second machine appeared at the other end of the street. The two helicopters faced one another, their black and gold Special Forces colours making them look like two giant wasps. Some kind of silent communication seemed to be going on between the machines. After half a minute, they floated up and turned in opposite directions to continue their search.

Sarah's senses told her that their pursuers had been fooled for the time being and passed on, but she and the others still waited an hour before they risked moving out into the street again.

Now what are we going to do? Nestor asked. The screen door of the florist's was jammed down, trapping the useless truck inside.

Sarah weighed the options in her mind. Find another vehicle that worked. Hide somewhere in the town and hope that somebody found them before HIDRA. Give up... She thought about Daniel lying in the back of the truck. He needed medical attention now the fall virus had put him into a coma – the kind that HIDRA could easily provide. Maybe it would be for the best if the helicopters did find them.

She became aware of the others standing around, waiting for her to say something. Nestor. Louise. Wei. Robert. They stood in a little semicircle by the side of the road, each looking tired and unwashed in the morning light.

They need me to tell them what's next, Sarah realized, feeling the weight of their expectation. Somehow she'd become their leader. She thought for a moment before speaking, remembering her conversation with Louise in the shop.

"We fight," she said.

The others looked at one another.

"If we run, we'll never escape those helicopters," she explained. "So we're going to make a stand here."

Wei gave a laugh.

"What, fight HIDRA?" he said. "All their soldiers and machines?"

"We did it before," Robert shot back at him, defending his sister. "They're afraid of us. I could tell back at the base."

"Me too," agreed Louise. "We can do it."

They all looked at Nestor, who had yet to speak. He shook his head.

"They're too strong," he said quietly. "There's too many of them."

"Please, Nestor," Sarah said. "We can do it. It's either that or give up now. Because we'll never make it otherwise."

He met her eyes, suddenly defiant.

I'm never going back to that base.

Sarah smiled and nodded. She sensed the resolve in the others.

"Okay," she said. "We don't know how long we've got, so we'd better get to work."

29

The first job was to search the buildings around the high street and find a safe place for Daniel.

In the end, they settled on an apartment above a shop selling tourist souvenirs and pieces of local art. It took the combined strength of Sarah, Nestor, Robert and Wei to carry him out of the truck, across the street and up the stairs to the bed they'd found. Louise held doors open for them. Along the way they dropped him a couple of times and one of his hands dragged along the ground for a little while before they noticed, but generally Daniel made it in one piece.

Sarah made sure Daniel was well tucked up before they left him. It was several hours since he'd succumbed to the virus, but she knew he would need medical attention within a few days if he was to survive. She didn't intend to be stuck in Esperinka that long, and Colonel Moss's forces were bound to find them before then anyway.

With Daniel sorted, they walked to a café across the street. The electricity wasn't working, but the large oven in the kitchen ran on gas. Sarah turned on one of the rings and reached for a box of matches on the workbench – it was empty.

Let me, a voice said at her side.

Sarah looked round to see Wei standing there. He pointed a finger at the hob and a single spark of fire ignited the gas. Wei held his fingertip to his mouth and blew on it with a grin.

"Thanks," Sarah said, putting down the empty box. "Your name's Sikong Wei, isn't it? Where have I heard that before?"

Wei cocked his head to one side and looked at her. "My dad is the manager of the McKeever–Sikong oil refinery. It's my grandfather's business."

"We were there," Sarah said slowly. "There was a massive fire. Do you know anything about that?"

She studied Wei's face, but he gave no response. Finally he said, "When the virus struck, someone must've had an accident."

With that, he turned and walked through to join Louise in the front of the café. They sat down at a table near the window and began talking quietly together.

"What was that about?" Nestor asked as he walked into the kitchen.

Sarah shrugged. "Possible fire hazard."

Nestor looked round at Wei and Louise. "You think he can't control his power yet?"

"I don't think any of us can," she replied, pulling a catering-sized tin of baked beans from the shelf and handing it to him. "Make yourself useful."

They set to work preparing the best meal they could. Twenty minutes later, they served plates of beans and tinned sausages. The five of them sat around the large table in the centre of the café and tucked into the food ravenously – it had been almost twenty hours since they'd last eaten.

As she wiped her plate clean with a piece of stale bread, Sarah looked round at the others. "Okay. Let's talk about how we're going to fight off Colonel Moss's men."

In turn they suggested how their powers might be used against any mirror-masks entering the town.

Louise's telekinetic ability – breaking glass, plastic and even metal – was an obvious choice against any vehicles they brought into town. The whirlwind that Nestor could conjure would provide a strong line of defence, especially when combined with Wei's pyrokinesis – the wall of fire had certainly worked back at the dome. Sarah was confident that her power of suggestion could be used to confuse or frighten away individual enemies, but she was unsure how effective they would be against two or more of the soldiers.

They talked for the best part of half an hour, each contributing ideas. As well as fighting off HIDRA, a clear priority was to find another vehicle that could get them out of the quarantine zone.

"Perhaps we could steal one of their helicopters!" Louise suggested.

Nestor raised an eyebrow. "And who's going to fly it?"

"Daniel showed you how to drive a truck, didn't he?" she said indignantly.

"Right," Nestor said, "I'm sure the controls are very similar."

At times they laughed and joked about some of the ways they could get the better of the HIDRA forces, forgetting that they were planning a war against the well-equipped task force heading their way. It almost seemed like a game.

But it wasn't a game. Sarah tried to remember that as she looked around the others.

Only Robert had been quiet during the discussion. She poked him in the arm and smiled in his direction.

Hey, are you okay? she asked so the others couldn't hear. Nestor had explained that by focusing on just one person, it was possible to have a conversation without the other mind-readers being able to pick it up. Telepathic instant messaging, Robert called it.

Yeah, he replied. *I mean, no. I'm the only one here without any powers.*

We're speaking using only our minds, Robert. What kind of powers do you want?

I mean, I don't have any extra-extra-special powers. I can't make windstorms or break stuff.

Sarah laid a hand on his shoulder, seeing how left out he felt.

Yours will come, I'm sure of it, she said. *I'm sorry if I've given you a hard time before. I haven't been very nice over the last few months.*

It's okay, Sarah. He smiled at her, but then his expression darkened. *How far do you think the fall virus has spread? Will there be more people like us?*

Sarah shrugged. *If there are, HIDRA will have something to worry about. And don't stress about not having a special power yet. I want you to be the lookout for the rest of us. That's the most important job. Find a way up on one of the roofs and keep an eye out for any trucks or helicopters. Think you can do that?*

Robert looked at her and nodded. The smile had returned to his face.

Sarah turned her attention back to the others.

"Okay," she said aloud, "so we all know what we can do. Now we have to get better at it. Everybody spread out and practise your skill, but be careful – give each other space. We don't need any injuries before the real battle. Robert is going to be the lookout. If he says they're coming, Nestor and Wei you're in charge of driving back the soldiers any way you can. Louise, you take care of any trucks that come in. I'll try my best to scare the living daylights out of anyone else."

The others nodded. For a moment, Sarah actually believed they had a chance.

30

They split up. If HIDRA entered the town she and her friends would be harder to fight if they were spread out, Sarah reasoned. She hoped she was right, as she'd also heard that there was safety in numbers. *I'm actually planning a battle,* she thought as she climbed the stairs to the apartment above the shop where they'd put Daniel. *Am I crazy?*

A window at the top of the stairs looked down onto the main street. Sarah paused there and took a moment to watch the others preparing themselves. Wei stood by himself at one end of the street. He pointed at a leaf blowing along the road and it spontaneously burst into flames. Nearer to the shop, Nestor sent a cloud of sand and dust whirling, forming a cloak that shielded him from her view within seconds. On the other side of the street, Louise held out a hand and a trash can began to rise into the air. She pushed out her arm and it flew down the street like a missile. Sarah turned towards the bedroom – it was her turn to get ready.

She looked at Daniel, sleeping so peacefully in the bed, and for a moment she almost envied him. He didn't have to fight any more. She quickly put that thought aside, however. They were going to send HIDRA packing and get out of Esperinka, not become slaves of Colonel Moss and his men. She'd already decided that when they got back to civilization, they'd help find the cure for Daniel and the other sleepers, but it would be on their terms – not HIDRA's.

She sat on the side of the bed and looked at his sleeping face.

"I'm sorry, Daniel," she whispered, pulling the sheet down a little. "I hope this doesn't hurt you, but I have to practise. They're relying on me to be strong."

Closing her eyes, she concentrated on the man sleeping in front of her, feeling out with her mind for his, making a connection. It was like pushing through layers of heavy curtain, feeling her way through to his dreams. After a few seconds she felt in contact with the tumbling, falling thoughts of the sleeper.

He stands in a desert that goes on for ever. In the distance smoke from a hundred oil fires stretches into the sky. As Sarah approaches he turns and smiles at her...

"Sarah! What are you doing here? Where are we?"

"Hi, Daniel. How are you feeling?"

"Okay, I guess. Is this a dream? It seems to have been going on for ever."

"Don't you remember what happened to you? The fall virus?"

He frowns. "Yes. Have you come to help me?"

She shakes her head. "We're going to fight Colonel Moss. He's chasing us and we can't get away, so all we can do is face them down."

Daniel nods his understanding. "So you came in here to test out your skills on me. Get a bit stronger."

"That's right," Sarah replies. "Do you mind?"

Daniel smiles. "How could I mind? Let me help."

"Okay. Tell me something that you're really afraid of."

Daniel thinks for a moment.

"Heights. I can't stand heights."

Sarah looks at the sandy ground surrounding them.

"Stand still," she orders.

The desert splits open around them and falls away, exposing giant chasms on either side. Simultaneously, the patch of ground on which they stand explodes upward, becoming the tip of a mountain stretching hundreds of metres into the air. Daniel struggles to keep his balance as he looks, wide-eyed, at the thousand-metre drop on every side. He meets Sarah's eyes and she sees real fear in them.

"Daniel..."

"Sarah! Well done! Don't stop! Show me what else you can do."

"You look kinda freaked out," Sarah says, suddenly worried about him.

Daniel waves a hand at her. "It's just like being on a rollercoaster. A really awful rollercoaster. Keep practising. You need to if you're going to beat them."

Sarah nods and brings the mountain they stand upon crashing to the ground. Around them she throws up a wall of fire that threatens to burn them to a crisp.

"Keep going!" Daniel cries above the flames, even as he cowers away from them.

Over the next hour Sarah puts them through more fire and ice, wind and rain. She covers Daniel in bugs and snakes and sends him to the top of the highest mountains.

Finally, wide-eyed and sweating, he holds up a hand for her to stop.

"That's enough, Sarah. I can't take any more. You're too strong now."

She steps forward to help Daniel as he falls to one knee, but she senses that he is already fading. He's drifting away from her into a deeper sleep, a place where she can't follow easily.

"Dad!" she cries out.

He smiles and touches a hand to her cheek. "Don't try to follow me, you'll never find your way back... Give Colonel Moss hell..."

He disappears before her...

In the apartment above the shop, Sarah opened her eyes and looked down at the sleeping figure of Daniel. He looked no different from an hour before. Except, as Sarah leaned closer, she saw that the corners of his mouth were turned up slightly in what might have been a smile. She suddenly wished more than anything that he was there to help them.

"We'll bring you back, Dad," she said. "We'll find a cure."

She turned away and walked through to the bathroom to stop herself from crying. She was suddenly flooded with rage at what had happened to them.

At what HIDRA wanted. Most of all, at Colonel Moss and the way he had treated them...

She splashed water on her face from the tap and looked into the mirror, wondering if she would look different from how she had a few days before. Older. What she saw made her jump back across the room.

Colonel Moss stood before her.

Sarah flew back, hit the shower curtain and almost fell into the bath. Opposite her, Colonel Moss jumped away in the other direction and was struggling to keep his balance. In confusion, she opened her mouth to scream for the others, but stopped as she realized that she was really looking in the bathroom mirror.

Regaining her balance, Sarah took a step towards the mirror, amazed at the sight of the colonel standing where her own reflection should have been. She raised a hand to her face and Colonel Moss did the same, wearing a shocked expression as he did so. Slowly, a grin spread across the reflection's face. The image of Moss was already beginning to fade and Sarah could see her own, normal appearance returning like a ghost through him.

Making sense of this new ability, Sarah tried to remember what she'd been thinking about as she walked through the bathroom door. *Colonel Moss, of course!*

She closed her eyes and brought Daniel to mind, trying to remember the details of his face and what he was wearing.

When she opened her eyes a few seconds later, her father stood before her. A perfect copy. Anyone looking at her wouldn't have been able to tell the difference. She looked down at her hands, which appeared large and manly and turned them over. It was as if she had been encased in the image of another.

"Hello?" she said aloud, experimenting, and was surprised to hear his voice emerge from her lips.

"Hi, I'm Daniel," she said, giggling a little at the deep sound coming from her throat.

When the image began to fade again, Sarah concentrated and brought it back, stronger, once more. She felt a little light-headed from the effort as she did so. She wasn't sure how long she would be able to keep up such a disguise without becoming exhausted, but was determined to find out.

With a shift of focus in her mind, the image began to change again, this time to that of a woman. Her mother stood before her in the mirror, looking young and healthy in a way that Sarah hadn't seen her for several years. The image smiled at her and she almost reached out to touch it.

"Mum!" came a cry from the doorway. A second later Robert threw his arms around her.

Sarah held him for a moment before pulling away. He looked up at her, his eyes filling with confusion as she allowed the illusion to fade away.

"But I thought I saw..." he began, his voice trailing off.

"I'm sorry, Robert," she said. "It's just a trick."

Something in his expression changed.

"I'm getting sick of the tricks," he said. "I'm getting sick of all your tricks. They're just making things worse."

Sarah reached out for him, but he moved away.

"You'd better come," he said, not looking at her as he went through the door. "Someone's trying to call us."

31

The sound of a telephone rang out across the high street. The others were already on the road as Sarah and Robert ran out. They all looked round, trying to work out where it was coming from.

"Over there!" cried Wei and pointed to the bakery across the road.

They ran over to the open doorway and piled into the building. The phone hung on the wall behind the checkout counter. They looked at it for a moment, nobody moving.

Sarah realized that everyone was waiting for her to do something, so she reluctantly walked around the counter. She reached for the receiver.

"Wait!" said Louise, making Sarah freeze. "Maybe it's a trick to see if we're here."

"I think they know we're here, Louise," Nestor said. "That's why they're calling."

"We could run," Wei suggested.

Robert shook his head. "Why don't they just leave us alone?"

Sarah thought about what her brother had just said. "That's a very good question, Robert," she replied. "And there's only one way to find out."

She picked up the telephone receiver and held it to her ear. "Hello?"

For a moment there was silence on the other end of the line, before a familiar voice spoke.

"Sarah. So nice to speak to you again."

It was Colonel Moss. She could recognize his soft, threatening tones anywhere.

"What do you want?" she asked.

"You've really done very well," he replied, ignoring her question. "Escaping from the base and getting as far as you have. You've led us quite a dance. But I think it's time that you gave it up, don't you?"

Sarah hesitated a moment before answering. Her first instinct was simply to hang up the phone. She realized Colonel Moss and his forces were probably circling the town at that very moment, preparing to attack. Yet, something told her that she might be able to gain something from keeping him talking just a little longer.

"Why don't you just leave us alone?" she replied. "None of us want to come back to the base. We're doing just fine by ourselves."

"Oh, I can see that," Colonel Moss replied with a laugh. "Hiding out in a ghost town with no way to escape. And then, of course, there's your father. How's Daniel doing, Sarah?"

Sarah bit her lip and closed her eyes, concentrating on the voice on the other end of the phone. She projected her mind across the distance linking her phone and the one Colonel Moss was holding.

"Well, Sarah?" Moss pressed. "Daniel needs urgent medical attention. The kind only we can give him."

Images began to form as Sarah felt herself making contact with Colonel Moss's mind. She felt his deviousness, the plans behind the words he was saying. He intended to take them back to the HIDRA base by any means necessary.

"You have to give yourselves up peacefully, Sarah,"

he continued. "You've got younger children with you. If my men have to come into town after you, I can't guarantee they're not going to get hurt. Sarah, are you listening to me...?"

She almost missed the question, so intent was she upon trying to read his inner thoughts.

"Yes," she replied hastily, trying not to lose focus, "how do I know we can trust you?"

"I give you my word..." Colonel Moss went on, his words fading away as Sarah went deeper into his mind. Now she was seeing into his memories: the first meteorite crash in Colombia and the survivors they found; discovering Nestor and Octavio's powers; Colonel Moss trying to force them to work for him, only Octavio fully obeying.

These images faded away as a more recent image began to take shape…

He watches through an observation window as Major Bright is being injected with a sample of the fall virus. Bright's eyes blaze fire and he bursts free of his restraints. The scientist standing over him backs away as Major Bright raises his hand. The room is engulfed as a maelstrom of swirling air sweeps the scientist away, along with the chair, the glass observation window, everything…

Major Bright stands in the centre of the destruction and smiles…

Concentrating harder, Sarah probed further ahead through the colonel's mind.

It is later. Major Bright is strapped down in a chair now, his body soaked with sweat, arms and legs trembling like a man with the flu. Beside him, one of the scientists tends nervously to the restraints holding him down.

"What's wrong with him?" Colonel Moss demands, grabbing the scientist roughly by his lapels. "Where is his strength?"

"He's going into withdrawal," the scientist stammers. "The powers he inherited from the blood samples are only temporary. He needs another injection of the serum."

"So give it to him!" Colonel Moss spits, waving to a rack of blood samples by the chair. "Give him enough to last him more than an hour this time!"

The scientist nods his head frantically. "Okay, but you must understand, we have limited samples from the children."

Colonel Moss sticks his face close to the scientist's. "So, replicate the serum."

"Not possible," the scientist replies. "The serum is created directly from the virus-enhanced blood. You need the children..."

"Sarah!" Colonel Moss's voice was suddenly sharp on

the other end of the line, cutting through the images, bringing her back to reality. "What are you doing? I feel..."

He needs us, she realized. *He needs our blood.* The thought sent a chill down her spine. As long as Colonel Moss wanted to create his super soldiers, they would have to live as his slaves – providing the raw material to make the serum.

"I saw what you did to Major Bright," she interrupted. "I know about the blood."

There was a silence on the other end of the line before Colonel Moss spoke again.

"Very clever," he said, all softness gone from his tone. "Your powers continue to surprise me. No one has ever been able to read me like that, not even Octavio. Perhaps you'll be even more powerful than him one day. If you survive this afternoon, that is."

"I know what you're planning, Colonel," Sarah pushed, sensing her advantage. "You won't use us to make soldiers. We've got rights and we're not going to be treated like that."

"Really?" Colonel Moss spat back. "I'm afraid that you're not going to have much choice in the matter..."

"We're not coming back, Colonel," she interrupted, deciding that she'd wasted enough time on him. "And if you want us, you'll have to come in here and get us."

"That's not—"

She cut him short by slamming the receiver down into its cradle.

"I guess we don't have to ask how that went," said Nestor.

"I hope you're all ready," Sarah replied. "They're going to be here soon. It's not too late to run. We could try to make it out of here on foot..."

The others looked at one another for a moment, a strange silence falling over the group. Wei was the one to break it. He held out his hand, fingers spread – in the centre of his palm a perfect sphere of fire appeared and grew until it was the size of a tennis ball.

I'm never going back to the base, he said as they watched, transfixed. *But I'm not running away either.*

With a sudden motion, he shot out his arm and sent the fireball flying. It smashed through the front window, flinging glass into the street.

I guess that means we're ready, said Sarah as they all looked at the Chinese kid in surprise. *Wei especially!*

He gave a shrug and they all laughed.

32

The Special Forces team entered the town from the south, skirting along the backs of the buildings rather than taking the high street.

There were four of them, all dressed in the lighter combat suits with their masks set to mirror-mode. Each soldier carried a dart-rifle with enough rounds to put a small town to sleep. Colonel Moss had briefed them that there were only five children to be captured.

It would be easy enough.

Moving in single file, the group commander led them

round the side of one of the buildings that looked onto the high street and motioned for them to halt for a moment. Sneaking a look around, he could see that the street was deserted. Clearly the children were hiding out in one of the shops.

"We'll sweep the buildings one by one," he ordered the three others through his intercom. "Dart-drop anything that moves. And I mean anything."

The others nodded their helmets as the commander moved into the centre of the road, keeping low and making for the florist's where the truck had crashed. More than likely they were still hiding inside, but you never knew. Halfway to the door, something happened that made him stop so quickly the soldier behind almost fell over the top of him.

Colonel Moss stood in the middle of the road.

The commander froze, motioning for his group to do the same as he blinked to make sure his eyes weren't deceiving him. He'd seen the colonel an hour before, when he'd briefed them about the mission back at the base. It didn't make sense that he was there, except...

"Don't ask questions," Moss barked at them, his voice strained and angry. "Just follow me."

Years of Special Forces training had taught the commander better than to disobey an order, especially when it came from Randall Moss. With a flick of his hand he led his men after the colonel, who ran down a side street near the florist's.

They found him standing beside an open cellar door at the rear of the building. Colonel Moss raised a finger to his lips as they approached.

"They're hiding down there, soldier," he whispered to the commander, pointing down into the cellar. "Take your men in and get them."

"All of us, Colonel?" questioned the commander, noticing for the first time that Moss wasn't wearing a protective suit in the contaminated zone. "Is that wise?"

"Just get down there and don't question me," Moss commanded, his voice raised. "They're sitting ducks!"

"Yessir!"

The soldiers primed their guns as the commander led them down the steps into the darkness. However, as the last man went down, they were surprised to find an empty room. Behind them, Colonel Moss swung the heavy steel doors shut at the top of the steps. There was a grating sound as an iron bolt was drawn across the door. A padlock clicked into place on the other side.

The commander ran to the top of the steps and threw his weight against the doors. They held firm. He turned to his men, who were standing at the bottom of the steps, looking up at him.

"Well, don't just stand there!" the commander barked. "Find a way out of here!"

After a few minutes of looking, he radioed the mobile base, one kilometre outside town.

"Uh, HIDRA base, this is Commander Green," he said sheepishly. "We've been trapped in a basement. By Colonel Moss."

Outside the building, Sarah ran back to the high street, allowing the image of Colonel Moss to fade away. Robert waved down at her from one of the roofs.

I got them! she called and he gave her the thumbs up.

Wait! he said. *I can see another group coming! From the north. There's five of them this time.*

Sarah nodded and concentrated again, allowing the image of Moss to surround her as she walked down the high street to meet the coming force. She tried to give herself a confident military strut.

The second wave of soldiers moved up the middle of the street in single file. Sarah held up a hand as they approached.

"Hold it!" she called in her most commanding colonel-voice. "You'd better turn back. It's not safe..."

The mirror-mask at the head of the column raised his

weapon without stopping to listen. Luckily for Sarah, he aimed at Colonel Moss's upper body because the two darts whizzed over her shoulder, embedding themselves in a nearby wall. Clearly her trick was only going to work once. Abandoning the pretence, she ran for the cover of the nearest building, diving through the door as a volley of darts struck the frame.

She hit the floor and looked round, seeing the group fan out around the front of the building, crouching low and training their weapons on the open doorway. Four of the mirror-masks began to advance on the shop, while a fifth made a run across the street. Sarah crawled back as a second round of darts was fired at the shopfront, shattering the glass. A dart hit the shop counter just a few centimetres from her head.

Nestor, make it fast! she thought desperately as she saw them aiming through the open window. On the other side of the street she saw Nestor appear from his hiding place and raise both his hands...

The sound of air howling began to grow outside, loud enough to make the mirror-masks pause for a second. The leader motioned for them to fire at the building again, regardless of the windstorm that was growing around them.

Another round of darts came through the window,

yet they never reached the target. As they flew towards her, Sarah saw them change course in the air under Nestor's control. They spun round and back towards the mirror-masks.

The soldiers scattered as they saw their own missiles being used against them, but it was too late. With great accuracy the darts pierced the protective suits of two of them. Within seconds they'd collapsed on the ground, guns falling from their hands. Nestor sent the darts that missed their targets back for a second try. One dart hit home, dropping a man, but a second was batted away by a soldier using his gloved hand. It shattered on the ground.

The mirror-mask who'd evaded his missile turned to Sarah and raised his dart-rifle, but checked himself, stepping towards the window before he fired. Clearly, he wanted to be sure his dart hit home. Sarah scrabbled towards the back door as the mirror-mask stepped cautiously through the window into the shop. Her sixth sense warned her of another attacker advancing from the rear. One of them had gone round the back.

Thinking fast as she entered the back room, Sarah cloaked herself in the image of one of her suited attackers. She found herself face to face with the mirror-mask who had broken away from the main group. The soldier who was following her from the front of the shop lowered his rifle in confusion as he came through the door. He turned from the disguised Sarah to the other mirror-mask and back again, unable to tell them apart.

"She's impersonating us!" Sarah shouted, aiming the imaginary gun she was holding at the man who had come through the back door. The soldier copied her and the two mirror-masks fired simultaneously, taking each other out. As they slumped to the floor, Sarah allowed her disguise to slip. She stepped over the nearest and walked out. At the front of the shop, Nestor was waiting for her.

"Are you okay?" he asked with concern. "I saw him go through after you."

"I'm fine," Sarah replied. "But that was too close for comfort."

Nevertheless, she felt a twinge of elation as she looked at the unconscious soldiers on the street around them. The feeling was short-lived, however.

They're coming again, Robert sent to them urgently. *This time they're bringing a tank.*

33

Two minutes later, the HIDRA tank rolled up the high street. It contained three soldiers and was armed with a water-cannon and gun turret that fired sleeping darts and stun-grenades.

Colonel Moss watched the scene from the safety of a helicopter hovering a kilometre outside town. He'd already lost nine of his men and he wasn't going to take any more chances. It was time for the heavy artillery.

The vehicle trundled up the street. However, the tank ground to a halt as the figure of a girl emerged from one of the buildings and walked to the middle of the road. Colonel Moss held the binoculars to his face, making out that it was Louise facing the tank. Beside him, Octavio strained to see without the aid of binoculars.

"My brother is down there," he said. "I can sense him."

Moss nodded and looked back to the scene unfolding in the distance.

"Engage the girl," he ordered through his communicator.

"Colonel?" the confused voice of the tank commander came back. "What should we do with her? She's eight years old!"

"Just take her down!" Moss spat into his intercom. "She's dangerous! But use non-lethal force. I don't want her damaged."

"Uh, yes sir..."

Through the binoculars Colonel Moss saw Louise raise her hand to the tank as the gun swivelled in her direction. The tank began to judder and vibrate on the spot. Seconds later, it imploded. It was as if the sides of the tank had been pushed inward by an unseen force. The metal crumpled like cardboard. Its suspension collapsed and the hatch on the top flew open. Suited soldiers piled out as the vehicle fell in on itself. Finally, it exploded as the fuel tank punctured.

Octavio raised an eyebrow. "Wow. She's getting powerful!"

"All units pull back!" Colonel Moss barked into his com.

Louise walked around the burning mass of the tank and held up both hands at the stunned soldiers. Their commander barked an order and the men fled the wreckage towards the edge of town. Louise lowered her hands.

"Dammit," cursed Moss, throwing down the binoculars and leaning towards the pilot of the helicopter. "Take us down there. We'll spray the whole town with sleep agent."

"Yessir," barked the pilot.

The helicopter went into a steep dive towards the main street. As they came within a hundred metres of the town the pilot threw a switch, releasing a cloud of sleep toxin from a tank on the underside of the machine. The pilot took them lower and covered the high street in clouds of the gas.

"Take us around again," Colonel Moss ordered and the helicopter was taken on a second pass. "All remaining units prepare for a full assault on the town..."

"Wait!" said Octavio, gripping Moss's arm. "It's not safe. I can feel it!"

Moss pulled away from the boy's grip.

"Take us lower!" he shouted to the pilot, who was beginning to struggle with the controls. A second later the machine spun violently, as if hit by a blast of air.

"It's Nestor!" Octavio yelled above the roaring of the wind. The helicopter was in the centre of a tornado and falling fast.

Colonel Moss reached desperately for a breathing mask, strapping himself in as he did so. The helicopter hit the ground. Its blades sheared off and the cockpit tumbled over and over. Glass smashed and Moss, Octavio and the pilot were thrown around violently until it finally came to a rest.

Although his head had been cut open by an impact against the window, Moss didn't waste any time. He grabbed a dart-gun from the wall and hauled open the broken door of the cockpit, dragging Octavio out with him as flames leaped up around the fallen vehicle.

"What about the pilot?" asked Octavio as he was dragged away.

"He just became dispensable," Moss replied harshly, pulling the boy over to the nearest building.

The helicopter exploded, showering debris around them.

"All units advance!" Colonel Moss yelled at the intercom attached to his shoulder.

The yellowish sleep gas hung in the air, but it was being quickly dispersed by the wind blowing around the buildings. Within seconds it was gone. Moss cursed and checked the dart-gun in his hand. He turned on Octavio.

"Why didn't you stop the helicopter from crashing?" he demanded. "Now your brother is blowing my sleep gas away. I thought you were meant to be more powerful than him!"

"I am!" protested Octavio. "He must have been practising..."

"I'm beginning to doubt your loyalty, Octavio," Moss said quietly. "You'd better do something to restore my faith in you. I'm starting to think you don't even have what it takes to be a soldier, let alone a leader."

The boy's eyes widened. "What can I do, Colonel?"

Moss nodded to the alley that led to the high street. "Go out there and get them. Do whatever you have to do with your powers. And by the way..." Moss grabbed Octavio's arm and pulled him close to make his point. "If Sarah doesn't make it, that's acceptable. The rest will be a lot easier to control without her in the future. Understand what I'm saying?"

As Colonel Moss released his arm, Octavio took a step backwards, remembering his last encounter with Nestor and the others.

"But there are five of them..."

Moss pointed the dart-gun at his head.

"That's an order, soldier," Moss hissed. "Don't come back until you've carried it out."

Octavio backed away, chilled by the coldness in the man's eyes. He knew better than to argue with Colonel Moss when he was in such a mood. He turned and walked towards the high street, away from his master.

Moss watched Octavio go, with a disappointed shake of his head. Suddenly he wasn't so convinced the boy's nerve would hold. Waiting until Octavio was out of earshot, he spoke into the intercom once more.

"This is Colonel Moss to mobile base," he barked into the com. "Let Major Bright off his leash. It's time to end this."

34

A duststorm whipped through the centre of town, cutting down visibility to a few metres. It was Nestor's work, providing cover for them to evade the mirror-masks who were moving along the high street. The wreckage of the tank was still burning, creating an obstacle for the soldiers to avoid as they advanced.

Sarah watched a group of three mirror-masks approach cautiously through the swirling dust, shielding her own eyes a little. Concentrating, she imagined a plague of locusts swarming towards them and they fell back in confusion at the unexpected sight. Pushing her advantage, she pictured the insects crawling inside their suits. One of them started clawing desperately at his suit, believing the locusts were crawling inside. Another ripped the helmet from his shoulders with a scream. Raising the dart-gun she'd picked up from one of the fallen soldiers, Sarah took aim and shot each one of them in turn. They fell where they stood.

Almost too easy.

On the other side of the street, Nestor was having similar success, driving another group back in the midst of a howling windstorm. As they desperately fired sleep darts in his direction, their missiles turned in the air and brought down each attacker.

Overhead, the whirr of a helicopter grew closer, invisible through the storm. Near the florist's shop, Louise raised her hands, her face strangely serene. Seconds later the helicopter engine spluttered and then died altogether as it was brought out of the sky.

At Louise's side Wei advanced. A line of flame shot forward under his control, blocking off the approach of another group. The fire shot under the body of a car and the fuel tank ignited seconds later. A plume of black smoke rose into the air. The mirror-masks backed away as the burning vehicle rolled over, nervously eyeing the other parked vehicles along the main street.

The mirror-masks who were still standing regrouped in the middle of the road. Crouching low, they conferred about the best course of action to follow. Sarah started walking towards them, dart-gun ready, as Nestor crossed from the other side of the road. On some unheard command from their leader, the group started to back away down the street, eventually turning tail and running. They were retreating!

Sarah looked around at the shattered buildings, the burning vehicles and the sleeping bodies of the mirror-masks, at least ten of them lying around on the street. She met Nestor's eyes and felt the same surge of elation in him.

They'd beaten Colonel Moss's men.

We did it! he said with a grin.

Sarah smiled back, but their celebration was cut short as a rumble went through the buildings lining the high street.

What's that? Nestor asked.

A force swept between them – sudden and powerful. Sarah cried out as she saw Nestor thrown back against the nearest building. He hit the ground and rolled forwards, dazed. Before she could make a move towards him, the air around her became a vortex of swirling dust, trapping her in the centre. With all her strength, Sarah threw herself forward and out of the tornado that was forming, hitting the ground hard. She rolled and raised the dart-gun, targeting the source of the attack. Octavio held up his hand as she fired twice. The darts ripped apart in mid-air before him.

Is that the best you can do? he asked with a sneer as Sarah lowered the weapon.

Nestor pulled himself to his feet and stumbled to her side. From across the street, Louise and Wei approached, hand in hand. Sarah looked round for Robert, but couldn't see him. She turned her attention back to Octavio.

"Still doing dirty work for Colonel Moss?" she shot back.

Octavio turned, trying to keep his eyes on all of them at once. Despite his bravado, Sarah sensed the fear in him.

"You know you can't take us all on," she said. "We've beaten you before."

Louise appeared at her side and scowled at the older boy. "I don't like you," she said dangerously. "I don't like you one little bit."

Octavio whitened a little and began to retreat along the street.

Why don't you just give it up? Octavio said with a

shake of his head. *You know that HIDRA will never stop chasing you. If you get away today, Colonel Moss will catch you tomorrow. Working with him is the only way. This is your last chance, Sarah. He wants you to join us.*

Why? To be his slave, like you?

She raised the dart-gun again, taking aim once more, but it flew from her hand into Octavio's. He turned it in his grip and took aim at her, but Nestor stepped between them, blocking his shot.

"Why don't we sort this out once and for all?" he said. "Just you and me."

A smile spread across Octavio's lips. He nodded and tossed the dart-gun aside.

Okay, but I warn you, Nestor: you know bringing a rain shower is no match for my telekinesis—

Nestor stepped forward without warning. He landed a punch squarely across his brother's jaw. Octavio's legs crumpled and he fell back onto the road. For a moment he lay on his back looking at Nestor, dumbfounded.

"Yeah!" Louise shouted across the street. "Go, Nestor!"

"Get up and fight me like we used to," Nestor demanded, gesturing for the other boy to get up. "No tricks."

With a cry of anger, Octavio flew up and ran at Nestor,

who dodged him easily and landed another blow on his cheek. Octavio spun round and hit the ground again. Nestor gestured for him to get up once more.

"Come on!"

Octavio dabbed at his split lip with a finger, but didn't move from the ground.

"You're a bully," Nestor said sadly, lowering his fists. "What happened to you?"

"I'm looking after us!" his brother spat. "One of us has to! Dad would have wanted me to be strong."

Nestor laughed. "And what do you think he would have thought of a man like Colonel Moss?" He waved his hand around the destruction in the town. "What do you think Dad would have said about all this?"

Octavio looked down, suddenly unable to meet his brother's eyes.

"Well?" Nestor demanded, real anger in his voice. "Don't you have anything to say?"

Octavio opened his mouth to say something but then closed it again. For once, he was lost for words.

Sarah moved to the fallen dart-gun and picked it up, keeping an eye on Octavio. Suddenly, with Nestor standing over him, he looked beaten – but she'd still be happier when he had a couple of sleep darts in his arm. She turned to take aim...

ALL OF YOU. STOP RIGHT THERE.

The voice cut through Sarah's mind like a knife. She could tell from the pained expressions on the faces of her friends that they'd heard it too. Even Octavio winced, looking back up the street to make out the source of the voice. It was like a hammer to their skulls, crude but full of power.

The dust cloud parted in the centre of the high street and a uniformed man strode through…

Major Bright.

Sarah and her group watched, frozen, as the soldier stopped beside Octavio. Major Bright looked different somehow, as if the muscles of his body were straining to break out from his uniform. It was his eyes, however, that were the strangest: they burned a terrifying red, making it difficult to hold his gaze. Sarah remembered her vision from Colonel Moss's memories and tried to focus her mind on Major Bright…

GET OUT OF MY HEAD! OR I'LL GET IN YOURS!

The words hit her like a brick wall and she staggered backwards. The sheer force of Bright's mind was terrifying. She found that she was trembling. Nestor placed a hand on her arm and met her eyes with concern.

"Sarah, are you okay?"

She shook her head. "They've done something to him. He's not normal any more. He has powers like us..."

They all looked back at Major Bright. Octavio struggled to his feet, wiping the blood from his mouth as he did so. A cruel smile passed across Bright's lips as he looked around at them.

WELL, WELL, WELL. YOU'VE HAD A GOOD RUN, BUT NOW IT'S TIME TO COME BACK TO THE HIDRA FOLD. YOU ALL HAVE SOMETHING I NEED...

His voice still screamed in their heads, as if he hadn't yet learned to control the volume, or didn't want to. A sheen of sweat stood out on his forehead and he grinned manically...

BLOOD...

If we work together, we can take him down, Sarah told the others. *We can combine our powers.*

A mocking laugh split her skull and Major Bright shook his head.

BUT SARAH, I ALREADY HAVE ALL YOUR POWERS. EACH AND EVERY ONE. WATCH!

Bright raised a hand and the dart-gun flew from Sarah's fingers and into his hand. He crushed the plastic frame with terrifying strength. Sarah and the others began to back away as he pointed at the ground. The tarmac of the road cracked and split. Major Bright raised his finger and the crack grew, splitting and growing until the entire road was breaking up down the centre.

"Sarah!" Louise cried out as a deep crevice split the street. The ground under her and Wei's feet crumbled and they fell down, into the chasm.

Sarah let out a cry and raced to the edge. Louise and Wei had fallen onto a ledge some ten metres below the street. Next to them, the crevice stretched down into the darkness.

"Don't move!" Sarah yelled down to them. "We're coming to get you!"

Louise nodded and Sarah turned her attention back to their attacker. Major Bright placed a hand on Octavio's shoulder. The boy stiffened and raised his hands.

What are you doing to me? Sarah heard Octavio ask, panic in his voice. He began to levitate, until he was hovering a metre off the ground under Major Bright's control. It seemed Octavio had finally met someone who was more of a bully than he was.

JUST HELPING YOU UNLOCK YOUR FULL POTENTIAL.

Bright directed his attention to Sarah.

LET'S SEE WHAT YOU CAN REALLY DO, OCTAVIO...

Octavio stretched his arms out in front, as if he had no control over his actions, his eyes blank and staring.

Sarah caught Nestor's arm as a howling sound filled the street. Before them, a swirling vortex began to appear. The dust from the air was being sucked up by a growing twister, spinning on the spot in the centre of the road. Second by second it grew, sucking in more dust until it was taller than the tops of the shops that lined the street. Octavio's face scrunched in concentration as he fed the whirlwind.

Octavio!

Nestor let out a cry of anger and rushed at his brother. Major Bright raised his free hand. Suddenly Nestor was lifted from his feet to hang in mid-air also, completely helpless.

YOU PICKED THE WRONG TEAM, NESTOR.

Nestor let out a cry of pain as his arms were pinned back by an unseen force. Sarah got to her feet and struggled forward against the growing power of the twister. She grabbed Nestor's legs and pulled him down with all her might. It was like prying him free of an invisible hand. Major Bright's laugh echoed through her mind.

OH, SARAH...

She looked up to see that the twister was now fully formed, massive and swirling with unreleased energy. Octavio trembled with the effort of keeping it under control. It was now that Bright pushed him roughly aside and took charge of the vortex. Exhausted, Octavio started to crawl away on the ground.

STAY WHERE YOU ARE, OCTAVIO. DON'T YOU WANT TO SEE YOUR BROTHER AND HIS FRIENDS BEATEN? WHEN I'M THROUGH WITH THEM, THEY'LL NEVER CROSS US AGAIN...

With a sweep of his hands, Major Bright sent the twister darting to the right. It collided with one of the shops and tore through the walls and roof. Bricks and glass flew through the air and were sucked into the tornado, feeding it. Major Bright drove it onwards and it ploughed through one building after another. It was then that Sarah saw Robert struggling along from roof to roof as he tried to escape the path of the destruction.

No! Sarah screamed. With a laugh, Major Bright pushed the tornado faster towards her brother.

Sarah ran forward, but Bright was too fast. Controlling the tornado with one hand, he shot out his other in her direction. His telekinetic force threw her against the smouldering wreck of the tank. She smacked hard against the metal and rolled over. Through watering eyes, she strained to see where the maelstrom was headed.

On the rooftops, Robert struggled to get as far away as possible from the raging twister. There was only one building separating him from it now. Finally, he found a way to jump onto a lower level and then leaped down into the street as the whirlwind ploughed through the shop behind him. Sarah breathed a sigh of relief as she saw him slide for cover beside an overturned car.

Octavio, help us!

On the ground, Octavio looked up at the sound of his brother's voice. Nestor was standing in the middle of the road, anger etched on his face.

Nestor, I didn't mean for you to get hurt, Octavio replied, struggling to his knees. *But he's too powerful.*

He's too powerful for one of us...

Nestor raised his hands, locking his eyes on the twister. Sarah watched as it slowly began to change course. It moved away from the shops and started coming back into the street. Concentrating on the whirlwind, Nestor forced it back in Bright's direction, his face contorted from the effort of fighting the Major's power.

Pulling herself up, Sarah ran forward. She placed her hands on Nestor's shoulders and concentrated her thoughts on him. She sensed the massive effort that he was making to keep control of the twister.

Nestor, don't give up, Sarah said as she felt him beginning to waver.

He's too strong, Sarah, Nestor replied. *I'm not going to be able to stop him on my own...*

She focused her thoughts on his mind and the struggle against Bright's power. Her own strength flooded into Nestor's mind and body, supporting him in his effort to wrest away control of the twister. Major Bright doubled his own effort – twisting his face into a mass of rage as he threw everything he had into driving the storm to crush them. The raging tornado spun ever faster between them as they poured in their energy. Sarah felt herself and Nestor beginning to weaken. At any moment Major Bright would break their defence and they would be engulfed.

A hand clamped down on Nestor's shoulder, adding a sudden surge of energy to their own, reviving them. Sarah looked round to see Octavio at his brother's side.

Don't stop now! Octavio's voice cried out in their heads. *We're stronger than him.*

What took you so long, brother...?

With those last words, Nestor pushed the twister with all his might towards Major Bright.

It swallowed him whole.

The whirlwind raged even stronger than before, expanding and turning blacker. Bright was caught in the centre of the vortex, massive forces distorting every fibre of his body. His clothes were in tatters and his skin ripped open in parts. For a moment Sarah thought they would see him torn limb from limb right there. There was an explosive sound, like the sonic boom of a jet aircraft as Nestor directed all of their power forward in one final effort.

NOOOOOOOOOOOOO!

Bright's inhuman cry of rage tore through their brains as the twister spun even more furiously, ripping through one of the remaining buildings and carrying on out into the desert under its own unstoppable power...

Nestor gave a cry of triumph:

Get lost!!!

Then, the twister was gone. The main street fell eerily silent.

Nestor slumped, exhausted, on the ground. Sarah and Octavio rolled him onto his back and kneeled over him. They stared at the spot where the twister had stood just a few seconds before. All that was left behind was a single item, torn from Major Bright's uniform: his name badge, bent and misshapen almost beyond recognition, lying in the dirt.

"Where did he go?" Octavio asked softly.

"He got carried away," Sarah replied.

A faint cry for help rang out nearby.

"Louise!" Sarah ran to the edge of the crevice. Louise and Wei huddled together on the crumbling ledge. Octavio appeared at her side and looked down.

"We have to help them!" Sarah exclaimed. The ledge looked on the verge of collapse.

Octavio nodded and stretched his hand over the edge. It was too far to reach, but that wasn't his intention.

You have to levitate, he called down to the girl. *I'll help you!*

Louise eyed him with suspicion.

"It's okay!" Sarah called back. "He's with us."

Louise nodded and wrapped her arms around Wei. Without warning the ledge gave way completely – but Louise and Wei didn't fall. Sarah looked round at Octavio and saw his face scrunched with concentration as he lifted Louise and Wei from the crevice with the force of his mind.

"That's it, Louise!" she called down. "Help him!"

Louise nodded with her eyes shut as they began to ascend from the pit. Seconds later they were close enough to reach. Octavio let out a breath and opened his eyes.

"Get them!"

They lunged forward. Sarah grabbed Louise and Octavio caught Wei. With effort, they pulled them out of the crevice and onto the road. For a moment, the four of them lay in a heap, trying to get their breath. Sarah lay on her back and looked at the dust parting overhead. She closed her eyes and gave a sigh of relief.

"I must say, that was spectacular," a voice said from the edge of the road. "I never thought you'd get the better of Major Bright."

Sarah turned to see Colonel Moss standing by the side of the ruined tank.

Locked in his arms was the struggling figure of Robert.

Colonel Moss had a gun pressed to his head.

35

The first thing Sarah noticed was that the weapon in Moss's hand was the type that fired bullets, not sleep darts. The threat to her brother was very real. The colonel saw the understanding in her eyes and smiled.

"I'm sure you realize that I'm not afraid to use this," he said to her as she and Octavio raised their hands. "If you try to get inside my head, I'm going to kill your brother right here in the street. And then I'll shoot you too. Let's keep this simple."

He turned his attention to Octavio.

"You're grounded. No more Xbox for a month."

Sarah suddenly felt more afraid than she had done during the entire attack on the town. She saw in Colonel Moss's eyes and sensed in his thoughts that he'd gone crazy. Before, he had wanted them alive to make more of the serum, but now he was even more dangerous: with Major Bright defeated, he would do anything to stop them from escaping the town and telling the world what they knew. He would take them alive if he could, but if not....

Who knows, Sarah thought to herself. *Amidst all this chaos, he might even get away with it.*

"All of you, on your knees!" Colonel Moss shouted, looking round at the buildings that had not been destroyed by the tornado. "Hands on your heads, or I'll start shooting."

I can stop him, Louise thought, meeting Sarah's eyes.

No! Sarah ordered. *It's too risky.*

Moss sensed the secret conversation passing between them.

"That's right, Sarah," he said as he moved closer to her, dragging Robert with him. "Tell them not to do anything stupid."

Do as he says, Sarah told the others and was relieved when they all obeyed. Only Nestor remained motionless, still unconscious on the ground following the fight against Bright.

Moss fumbled for the intercom on his shoulder.

"This is Colonel Moss," he hissed urgently. "I have the targets contained. Get back in here."

Sarah met Robert's eyes and she could see the fear in them.

I'm sorry, Sarah, he thought. *I tried to get away, but he was too fast.*

It's okay, she replied. *We're not going anywhere with him.*

Robert nodded. *I think I can help...*

Don't do anything silly...

There's something I've been practising. Haven't got it to work properly yet, but maybe now I've got no choice... Just get ready to run...

Robert closed his eyes, concentrating. Colonel Moss looked down at the boy, as if sensing something was up.

"Wait, what are you doing?" he demanded.

And then Robert disappeared.

Moss stumbled backwards, shocked to find his arms suddenly empty. Sarah gasped and looked around, desperately searching for her brother.

"Robert!" she cried out loud.

Over here, Sarah!

Sarah spun round as he blinked back into existence a few metres away from Moss. The colonel raised the gun reflexively, firing a round with an ear-splitting roar. But Robert had already disappeared again, this time reappearing beside a stunned-looking Louise.

Run! Sarah screamed to the others and they scattered. Octavio headed for the semi-conscious Nestor, dragging him towards one of the remaining buildings. Robert grabbed Louise and Wei, while Sarah sprinted for cover behind the shattered tank.

A bullet whizzed past her head and she realized that Moss had fired again. She stumbled and hit the ground, tumbling over. She waved the others on into the shops as she struggled to her feet, making to follow them.

"Hold it!" Moss barked, stopping her in her tracks. She turned to see him levelling the gun at her head.

"I don't think any of you are strong enough to stop a bullet, do you?" he said quietly. "Yet."

Sarah backed away slowly in the direction of the florist's. Colonel Moss followed, matching her pace.

"Was all this worth it?" Sarah asked, gesturing around the wreckage of the town and the unconscious Special Forces soldiers. "You just saw your second-in-command destroyed. Your Superhuman project is over.

And all you have left is a gun in your hand."

Moss shrugged.

"There's a price to pay in any battle," he replied. "Major Bright was a pioneer. One day everyone's going to want to have powers like you and your friends. Everyone you meet from now on is going to want to know your secret, just like me. I can protect you all, Octavio knows that. Or, at least, he did."

"Protect us?" Sarah repeated with a laugh. "By keeping us in cells for the rest of our lives? Farming our blood to make serum?"

"Well, there has to be give and take," Colonel Moss said. He shifted his grip on the pistol as he got closer. "I give you protection and you give me power."

Sarah stopped walking, sensing that he was actually about to fire the weapon.

"You have to stop this," Sarah ordered him, her voice full of authority. *PUT THE GUN DOWN.*

Moss blinked and shook his head, as if trying to clear his thoughts. A smile spread across his lips and he raised the gun again.

"Nice try, Sarah," he spat, "but I've spent enough time with Octavio to not be easily controlled."

Sarah continued backing away, her heart sinking a little. Then she sensed something unusual happening in the florist's where they'd left the truck. Moss continued his advance.

"I'm not going anywhere with you, Colonel Moss," she said finally. "I don't like being told what to do. You'll just have to shoot me. *If you can*."

Moss grinned. "I've done worse in my time, believe me. Normally, I wouldn't destroy such a precious commodity, but since we picked you up, you've been nothing but trouble. Too much trouble."

Sarah could feel the colonel's finger tense on the trigger...

"Hopefully the others will be more cooperative," he spat.

Moss was going to do it...

Sarah sensed something else...

She threw herself to the right...

The metal screen covering the front of the florist's shop exploded as the HIDRA truck flew out at high speed. Moss cried out, spinning round and managing to fire off three shots before the back of the vehicle hit him full on, sending him tumbling back across the street. He landed in a crumpled heap, the gun flying from his grasp.

Sarah looked round at the truck as it ground to a halt. The cab door opened and Robert jumped out. She ran over, throwing her arms around him and crying with relief.

"How did you manage to drive that thing?" she asked as the others appeared from the wreck of the florist's and gathered round.

"Louise gave me a push," he said with a grin. Sarah looked round to see the younger girl standing by the side of the road.

"Is he dead?" Louise asked, looking over at the fallen body of Moss. Octavio left his brother and went over to check the colonel's pulse.

"No, he's alive," he said. "What shall we do with him?"

Sarah thought it over. She looked at the twisted remains of the tank and a grin spread across her face.

36

From her cell, Dr. Rachel Andersen listened to the sound of sirens and vehicles leaving the base. After a while, everything went quiet. She sat on her bed and looked at the wall. The end couldn't be too far away. Colonel Moss would send someone for her and that would be it. He had full control of HIDRA, but he couldn't let her tell the world everything she knew. The cover-up would involve her being *relocated* to a grave in the desert, no doubt – like he'd tried to do with Daniel Williams.

Eventually, footsteps approached the door.

"Dr. Andersen?"

She looked round at the soldier who was standing in the doorway and mentally prepared herself. She rose and faced him.

"Okay, let's get this over with," she said, looking at the pistol on his belt. "I know why you're here. I guess Colonel Moss really doesn't like to get his hands dirty if he sent someone else to finish me."

The soldier frowned at her, confused.

"Colonel Moss is missing, ma'am," he said. "We lost radio contact with him two hours ago. Major Bright as well."

Rachel blinked at him, trying to make sense of what she was being told. For the first time she registered that the man standing before her wasn't dressed in a Special Forces uniform – he was normal HIDRA.

"The colonel took his men into Esperinka after the escapees," the soldier went on. "There's no one in charge here, miss. As you're the most senior officer, General Wellman ordered that you should take control. In fact, he's on the satellite phone from Paris right now."

Rachel nodded, finally pulling herself together. She noted the name badge on his chest – *Lieutenant Viktor Kaminski*. He offered her the sat phone.

"The general only wants to speak to you, ma'am."

"Okay, Kaminski," she said, "fuel me up a truck and load it with supplies. You've got ten minutes."

The lieutenant saluted snappily and ran from the room.

"General Wellman," she said into the phone.

The voice on the end was urgent. "Dr. Andersen, I don't know what the hell Colonel Moss has been up to, but I'm relying on you to put it right..."

The sun was setting by the time they approached Esperinka. Rachel peered through the filthy windscreen at the smoke rising from the town in the distance.

"Dr. Andersen!" Lieutenant Kaminski exclaimed as he put his foot on the brake.

On the side of the road a line of mirror-masked soldiers was walking in the opposite direction. Their suits were dirty and torn in places, but all bore the unmistakeable black and gold insignia of Colonel Moss's Special Forces. Many of them were injured.

Rachel checked the sensor on the dash of the truck. Its display indicated that the air outside the vehicle was no longer contaminated by the airborne virus. The dust had settled. She pulled off her protective mask and rolled down the window of the truck so she could talk to one of the passing soldiers.

"What happened?" she called out to him.

The man looked up at her and flicked off mirror-mode on his helmet. His face looked exhausted, beaten.

"The colonel said there were only five of them," he said with a shake of his head. "It was like going up against an army..."

"Where's Colonel Moss?"

The soldier shrugged. "Back there. Major Bright is... somewhere. I wouldn't go into that town if I were you."

"Carry on up the road," she said. "More relief trucks are on the way. And tell your men they can take off their helmets. The contamination period is over."

Rachel motioned for the driver to carry on and they left the soldiers behind. Closer to the town they passed the smouldering wreckage of a helicopter. Kaminski shot her a look.

"It's okay," she reassured him. "Just try not to look threatening."

The driver swallowed and pulled the truck onto the main street. Slowly. The wreckage of the tank stood in the centre of the road. Only a few buildings from the main street were still standing. The rest were little more than broken frames now, as if they'd been through a hundred years' worth of storm damage in one day. The road was torn open, looking like an earthquake had hit. Rachel signalled for Kaminski to stop as she noticed someone sitting beside the tank. Colonel Moss.

"Wait here," she ordered Kaminski as she jumped out of the cab. "Don't do anything stupid."

"Don't worry," Kaminski replied, scanning the devastated high street nervously.

Rachel walked towards Colonel Moss. The torn metal of the tank had been twisted and wrapped around his wrists so that he was held securely. It would take a metal-cutter to get him free. Rachel wondered what force could have manipulated the steel in such a way. *Louise.*

Moss's eyes, still full of rage, followed her as she approached. He said nothing. What looked like a handkerchief had been stuffed in his mouth and secured with tape. Rachel stopped in front of him and bent to remove the gag.

"Don't do that."

Rachel turned to see Sarah standing by the side of the road.

"Take that out of his mouth and I guarantee you'll want to put it back in again in two minutes flat," she said. "He just won't shut up."

Colonel Moss strained against his bonds and made a muffled whining sound against the gag. Rachel thought that Sarah probably had a point. Moss had said enough.

"What happened to Major Bright?" she asked.

Sarah looked up and waved her hand through the air. "Swept away. Into the desert. You might want to send some men to pick up what's left."

Rachel nodded. The girl seemed different to the last time she'd seen her. There was no fear in her now.

"I'm in control of HIDRA," she told Sarah. "It's safe for you to come back with me."

Sarah held her eyes for a moment.

"Safe?" she said with a smile. "You mean you won't perform any more tests?"

"Not unless you want me to."

"Why would I want you to?"

"We still have to find a cure for the fall virus, Sarah," Rachel said, moving towards the girl. "I can make things different. We can save a lot of people."

She froze as Sarah produced a dart-gun from the back of her jeans and held it up.

"That's far enough. I know you have good intentions, Rachel. I can read you. But what about in the future? When HIDRA puts another Colonel Moss in charge? When they reboot the weapons programme?"

"It won't happen again."

Sarah shook her head. "You can't guarantee that."

You're right, I can't, Rachel thought. She looked around the ruins of the high street.

"Where are the others?" she asked. "Don't you think they should be given the chance to decide for themselves?"

Sarah looked over her shoulder. If she spoke to her companions, Rachel didn't hear it.

They emerged from one of the remaining shops. Rachel cast her eyes over the children who used to be HIDRA's prisoners. They were bedraggled and looked as if they hadn't bathed in a year, but they stood tall behind Sarah. She was surprised to see Octavio among them.

"They've already made their decision," Sarah replied. Behind her, the others stood as one.

Rachel realized there would be no arguing with them, so she decided not to even try. She pointed at the truck she'd arrived in.

"There's food and medical supplies in the back," she told them. "Plus something to help Daniel. Keep driving east and you'll hit the edge of the quarantine zone within an hour. I'll radio ahead. They won't try to stop you."

Sarah looked at her sceptically.

"Special Forces aren't in control any more," Rachel assured her. She pulled a mobile phone from her pocket and handed it to the girl. "Take this. Just in case you want to get in touch in the future. My number's in there."

Sarah turned the phone over in her hand before putting it in her pocket. "Thanks. I'd like to come with you, Rachel, but HIDRA has a long way to go before any of us trust it again. Okay?"

Rachel nodded and took a final look at the children standing before her.

"Congratulations," she said. "You did us all a service today."

With that, she turned and started walking back up the street. The only sound was the muffled howls of protest from Colonel Moss.

"Get out, we're walking," she ordered Kaminski when she reached the truck. "Radio the dome and tell them to send some transport to pick us up."

"What about Colonel Moss?" asked the lieutenant as they walked out of town.

"We'll collect him later," Rachel replied. "When we clear up the rest of the trash."

They followed the path of the other soldiers back towards the base. After five minutes of walking Rachel stole a look back at the town.

The truck was gone.

37

They drove east.

Octavio took the wheel and he proved to be pretty good at it. Like Nestor, his legs were long enough to reach the pedals with ease. Louise and the others still looked at him without much trust, so he was glad of something useful to do.

The radio started broadcasting again. It gave advice on the locations of medical camps for people searching for friends and relatives. All over the neighbouring states, a mixture of Australian and international aid forces continued to care for the sleepers. It seemed that the spread of the virus had been limited to the quarantine zone, so HIDRA had managed to do one thing right. Nevertheless, over five thousand people had been affected by the fall virus within the zone.

Robert sat alongside Octavio as they bounced along, but after a while got bored. He thought of the others in the back of the truck and teleported there instantly.

"Hey, you're supposed to be keeping an eye on Octavio!" Sarah said as he appeared beside her.

"He's fine," Robert replied, looking down at Nestor, who was lying on a stretcher. "How is he?"

"Sleeping," Sarah replied. "Exhausted."

"And Daniel?"

"He's doing good too," Sarah reassured him.

She looked round at the sleeper casket hanging from the roof – it now contained their father. The read-outs on the side showed that he was in a perfectly stable sleep. The machine could keep him like that for years to come. Or until they found a cure.

Hey, Octavio called to them from the front, *it's the HIDRA checkpoint!*

Sarah and the others crowded forward to the window that looked into the cab. Through the front they could see the truck fast approaching a boom gate that had been set up across the road. Beside the gate, two soldiers in HIDRA uniforms waved at them to slow down. Sarah's heart leaped. It was the edge of the quarantine zone. Beyond was freedom.

I'm braking, Octavio said.

Put your foot down! Sarah commanded. *Smash through that gate!*

But Dr. Andersen said...

Sarah sighed. *When are you going to stop listening to what they say at HIDRA, Octavio?*

He only hesitated for a moment.

Okay...

The truck picked up speed as he pressed his foot down on the accelerator. Ahead, the soldiers started to wave even more frantically.

The truck smashed through the gate, splintering it into a million pieces.

Inside the truck, everyone cheered as they sped out of the quarantine zone. Sarah looked out the back at the wrecked HIDRA checkpoint and the shouting soldiers as they receded into the distance.

Goodbye, HIDRA.

The road to Melbourne stretched ahead of them.

* * *

They weren't there yet, however. A stolen military truck containing six kids and a sleeper casket could attract a lot of attention. The roads were clogged with convoys of aid and rescue vehicles. Sarah wasn't ready to answer questions until she'd decided what they were going to do.

So, taking the map, she sent them south, towards the coast. It was the long way round, but the others didn't argue. They were just happy to be away from HIDRA.

On the second day, they reached the ocean.

Octavio pulled the truck into a car park and they piled out of the vehicle, running to the edge of the cliffs that overlooked a series of massive rocks standing out to sea.

"The Twelve Apostles," Sarah told the others. "I read about these back in England."

They found a way down the cliffs to the beach. Robert, Louise and Wei ran around, enjoying their hard-earned freedom. Every now and then Robert would disappear, then reappear somewhere else. The others would chase after him in an unconventional game of tag. Octavio stood quietly off to the side, looking out across the water.

"He'll be okay," Sarah said, seeing Nestor looking with concern at his brother.

"He feels guilty," he said. "Helping the colonel."

"He just needs time."

Nestor nodded and walked down the beach to join Octavio. Robert appeared by her side. Literally appeared.

"What's up with those two?" he asked, looking at the Colombian twins walking by the water's edge.

"They've got some stuff to talk about," Sarah replied as Robert sat down beside her. She took the mobile Rachel had given her from her pocket and unclipped the back. She removed the sim card and replaced it with Daniel's. When the card loaded she searched the memory for the name of his contact – Alexei.

"Who's that?" Robert asked.

"The guy who's going to take the diamonds off our hands," she replied. "Daniel said he's trustworthy."

Robert detected the uncertainty in her voice and looked at her questioningly.

"You think he'll try to double-cross us?" he asked.

"More fool him if he does," Sarah answered with a grin. Her real concern was the idea of using the diamonds full stop. She seriously doubted they would bring any good in the long run, but she knew they had no choice. If they wanted their freedom, they would need money. Sarah keyed in a text message: HAVE PCKAGE – ON ROUTE TO MEL. Allowing herself just one more moment of hesitation, she pressed *send*. It was done.

The sun came out, warming them despite the sea breeze. Waves rolled around the massive pillars of rock known as the Apostles, sending up crashing sprays of foam. The noise was deafening. Moments later, Wei and Louise came running with a handful of iced lollies from the gift shop at the edge of the car park.

"The woman in the gift shop gave us these," Louise explained breathlessly. "She started asking questions about the truck, so we told her we're on a day trip from the medical base."

"Very smart," Sarah said as Wei handed a lolly each to her and Robert before running over to the twins.

"What are we going to do, Sarah?" Robert asked finally.

She looked out to sea. It was the question that had been haunting her since they'd left Esperinka. *What are we going to do?* she thought.

"We stay together," she decided. "Rachel was right. We do hold the secret to a cure and we can save Daniel and the others. But we're going to do it on our terms, not HIDRA's. People will want our power, so we've got to be careful who we trust."

"We need to find Louise and Wei's parents," Robert added.

Sarah nodded. "We'll find them, and we'll find the cure for them too."

The phone in her hands vibrated and she opened a new message: LETS MEET. She snapped the phone shut and put it in her pocket. Robert looked at her questioningly.

"Think we've got a buyer," she said and immediately felt another pang of doubt, but she didn't let it show this time. She'd made her decision to use the diamonds and would follow it through – there was no use in worrying Robert. She changed the subject by placing a hand on his shoulder and saying, "I'm glad you finally found your power. It's pretty cool."

Robert smiled, throwing his arms around her unexpectedly. *I'm glad too*, he said, just before he disappeared from her arms, reappearing ten metres up the beach. *But I bet you can't catch me!*

Checking no one was watching from the cliff tops, Sarah chased after him with a laugh and soon the others joined in as well, even Octavio. As the waves crashed, they chased up and down the beach happily. Robert teleported from one spot to another and Nestor whipped up the sand in great clouds.

Finally, exhausted, they fell down on the sand and watched the sun set slowly in the west.

Epilogue

The HIDRA staff car pulled onto the deserted sixth level of the multi-storey car park and circled round in the middle before stopping. In the driver's seat Lieutenant Kaminski scanned the area unhappily and turned to the passenger in the back.

"I don't like this, Colonel," he said. "Something's wrong."

Rachel Andersen put her hand on the door. "Just keep the engine running."

Kaminski held out a dart-gun in her direction,

handle-first. "Just a precaution, ma'am."

"If I'm carrying that, I really will be in danger," Rachel replied with a shake of her head.

She stepped out of the vehicle, pulling her coat tight against the chill of the night air. Glancing around, she saw what she was looking for – a white X chalked on one of the support pillars. The lights beyond had been knocked out, creating an area of darkness that was hard to penetrate even with her keen eyes. She walked in that direction.

"Hold it!" a familiar voice called from the shadows. "That's far enough, Colonel."

Rachel stopped and held up her hands. "Sarah?"

"So, you're military now?" Sarah responded, emerging from the darkness. "Just like Colonel Moss."

Rachel shook her head. "Just an honorary title as I'm still a civilian. They put me in charge of HIDRA operations in the Asia-Pacific region. Under my command, the soldiers answer to the scientists."

"For now," Sarah added, studying Rachel closely.

"My superiors have learned their lesson," she said. "Moss has been flown back to Europe under guard. He's going to be court-martialled."

Sarah frowned. "I doubt that very much and so do you. They'll bury the story. Make him disappear."

Rachel realized that there would be no hiding things from Sarah now. Her mind was an open book to the girl.

"HIDRA can't afford to be associated with a madman like Colonel Moss," Rachel admitted. "But I promise he'll be locked up where he can never harm anyone again."

"And HIDRA goes on as normal."

"We're the only ones in a position to fight the fall virus," Rachel insisted. "We contained it here in Australia, but what if another meteorite lands near a city? We've also just heard about the outbreak of a fall-like virus in a remote part of Russia – origin unknown. This isn't over. You and the others hold the key to the cure. You need to come in with me..."

Sarah shook her head slowly. Rachel sensed the presence of others standing in the shadows for the first time – the five other children listening to their conversation intently.

"You must help us!" Rachel protested, looking around the darkness.

Sarah gestured behind her and was handed an object – a red, plastic case. She bent down and slid it across the ground to Rachel.

"We want to find a cure just as much as you do,"

Sarah said as Rachel picked it up. "We'll help, but want some things in return."

Rachel opened the case. Inside were six vials – each containing a blood sample and labelled neatly with the name of a different member of Sarah's group. Rachel pulled out the one marked *Louise* and wondered how they'd managed to...

"We used the blood tester kits from the truck you gave us." Sarah answered her question before it was voiced. "Those samples should keep you going for now. Plenty of information for your people to process."

Rachel nodded. The snapshot of the evolving virus the samples would provide would be invaluable. She replaced the vial and closed the lid of the case.

"What do you want?" she asked. "Money?"

Sarah smiled, as if the question was a stupid one. "We're doing just fine, thanks. What we need is information. Like what happened to Louise and Wei's parents for a start."

"Moss and his men displaced a lot of people," Rachel replied. "We're still trying to piece together everything they covered up—"

"Then try harder," Sarah interrupted forcefully.

Rachel nodded. "How will I—"

"We'll contact you," Sarah replied. She tapped her

forehead. "Until then, we'll be listening. If we find out HIDRA is pursuing the weapons programme with those samples, you'll answer to us."

She stepped back into the shadows and Rachel sensed the others moving away.

"Wait!" she exclaimed. "There's something else – my men never located Major Bright's body in the desert."

Sarah looked back and nodded. "We know," she said. "There's a chance he's still out there. But when we find him, you'll be the first to know..."

Rachel moved forward quickly, reaching out to the girl. "Sarah, come back with me..."

Sarah held up a warning hand. "Louise!"

The front and back tires of the HIDRA car exploded simultaneously. Kaminski jumped from the vehicle, a weapon in his hand. Rachel turned and waved him away.

"Lieutenant, stay where you are! Sarah, it's okay."

But when Rachel turned back, she sensed only darkness before her. Sarah and the others had melted away into the night.

With a sigh of resignation, Rachel tucked the case of blood samples under her arm and walked through the shadows to the low wall overlooking the night sky of Melbourne. In the distance an ambulance siren howled through deserted streets. The drone of a helicopter sounded overhead and Rachel watched its lights travel through the night sky in the direction of the new HIDRA base on the outskirts of the city, wondering if it was one of theirs. She turned her attention back to the streets.

Sarah and the others were out there somewhere.

"Good luck," she said, before turning and walking back to the car.

Sarah's team is in hiding...

...and they're not the only ones. Granted the power of invisibility by the fall virus, Alex has committed one bank robbery too many – now the police are on his trail. And somewhere out in the desert, an old enemy is biding his time...

But from the distant wilds of Russia comes an unexpected offer of help. A mysterious stranger claims to know the truth about the virus. But the truth can be a very dangerous thing.